W9-APF-358

"Grant, I owe you—"

"Nothing." He cut her off, actually sounding as though he meant it. "You owe me nothing."

She snorted. "I owe you a lot more than just an apology. I wish I could go back to the day Clive asked me if I wanted to take time off from SWAT and—"

"Stop it," Grant said, and it wasn't his words but the fact that he put his finger over her lips that silenced her.

The touch sent a tingling feeling over her face, and he must have seen something in her eyes, because his expression changed, too. The serious veneer was gone, replaced by a mixture of emotions she couldn't begin to unravel. But worry and desire were definitely part of the mix.

His gaze dropped to her lips, and instead of moving his finger, he traced it slowly over her mouth.

Her entire body suddenly seemed to come alive as the tingling swept outward, down to her toes. She stepped back fast. "What are you doing? I got you *shot* today!"

Dear Reader,

Thank you for coming along with Maggie as she finally faces down the demons of her past with the help of her SWAT teammate Grant. I hope you also enjoyed getting to know Maggie's brother, Scott, and their friend Ella. *Disarming Detective*, the first book in The Lawmen series, followed Ella as she met her match in Florida police detective Logan Greer. Last month, the series continued with *Seduced by the Sniper* as Scott met the one woman who could convince him to think beyond one date; unfortunately, she was also the only witness to a massacre and under his protective custody.

If you've enjoyed my Lawmen books, I hope you'll also look for *Hunted* and *Vanished*, the first two suspense novels in my Profiler series from MIRA Books, out now. *Hunted* introduces FBI profiler Evelyn Baine as she tracks down a notorious serial killer dubbed the Bakersville Burier. In *Vanished*, Evelyn may finally have the chance to unravel what happened to her best friend, who disappeared eighteen years ago—as long as the Nursery Rhyme Killer doesn't make Evelyn vanish without a trace, too.

If you'd like more information about upcoming releases, events and extras—and to sign up for my newsletters for release reminders—please visit me at elizabethheiter.com.

I love hearing from readers!

Elizabeth Heiter

Acknowledgments

Thank you, as always, to my friends and family for your support. A special thanks to Chris Heiter, Robbie Terman, Ann Forsaith, Nora Smith, Charles Shipps and Sasha Orr, for your feedback, and Mark Nalbach, for keeping my website going.

Thank you to my agent, Kevan Lyon, and my editor, Paula Eykelhof, for always pushing me, and to Denise Zaza and everyone on the Intrigue team, for all your help behind the scenes. A big thank-you as well to the Intrigue authors, for the friendly welcome—I love being in your company.

SWAT SECRET ADMIRER

ELIZABETH HEITER

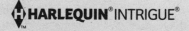

If you purchased this book without a cover you should be aware that this book is stolen property. It was reported as "unsold and destroyed" to the publisher, and neither the author nor the publisher has received any payment for this "stripped book."

For my critique partner, Robbie Terman.
Thank you for convincing me
that I could write romantic suspense,
and lending your expertise.

ISBN-13: 978-0-373-69827-1

SWAT Secret Admirer

Copyright © 2015 by Elizabeth Heiter

Recycling programs for this product may not exist in your area.

All rights reserved. Except for use in any review, the reproduction or utilization of this work in whole or in part in any form by any electronic, mechanical or other means, now known or hereinafter invented, including xerography, photocopying and recording, or in any information storage or retrieval system, is forbidden without the written permission of the publisher, Harlequin Enterprises Limited, 225 Duncan Mill Road, Don Mills, Ontario M3B 3K9, Canada.

This is a work of fiction. Names, characters, places and incidents are either the product of the author's imagination or are used fictitiously, and any resemblance to actual persons, living or dead, business establishments, events or locales is entirely coincidental.

This edition published by arrangement with Harlequin Books S.A.

For questions and comments about the quality of this book, please contact us at CustomerService@Harlequin.com.

® and TM are trademarks of Harlequin Enterprises Limited or its corporate affiliates. Trademarks indicated with ® are registered in the United States Patent and Trademark Office, the Canadian Intellectual Property Office and in other countries.

Printed in U.S.A.

™ www.Harlequin.com

Elizabeth Heiter likes her suspense to feature strong heroines, chilling villains, psychological twists and a little romance. Her research has taken her into the minds of serial killers, through murder investigations and onto the FBI Academy's shooting range. Elizabeth graduated from the University of Michigan with a degree in English literature. She's a member of International Thriller Writers and Romance Writers of America. Visit Elizabeth at elizabethheiter.com.

Books by Elizabeth Heiter

HARLEQUIN INTRIGUE

The Lawmen
Disarming Detective
Seduced by the Sniper
SWAT Secret Admirer

MIRA

The Profiler
Vanished
Hunted

CAST OF CHARACTERS

Maggie Delacorte—FBI SWAT agent who hasn't let any man get close since a brutal abduction by the infamous Fishhook Rapist a decade ago. Teammate Grant Larkin can't be the exception, especially not with the anniversary of her assault fast approaching, and her abductor vowing that this time, there's no coming back.

Grant Larkin—He's had feelings for Maggie since he joined her SWAT team, and he'll do anything to keep her safe—including work on her case against her wishes. But the closer he gets to solving the case, the more he may be pushing Maggie away.

Scott Delacorte—Maggie's overprotective older brother. A decade ago, he and Maggie—along with best friend Ella Cortez—made a pact to join the FBI. With the anniversary coming up, Scott is sticking close, but he's worried the Fishhook Rapist could outwit them all.

Ella Cortez—One of Maggie's best friends. A decade ago, she, Scott and Maggie made a pact to join the FBI. Now she's standing by Maggie, but will that put her in the line of fire?

The Fishhook Rapist—He targets one woman a year, then releases her, branded with a permanent reminder on the back of her neck. A decade ago, Maggie was his first victim, and now he's decided to return for her one last time.

Clive Dekker—Maggie and Grant's boss on SWAT. It's up to Clive to decide whether Maggie's too distracted by the Fishhook Rapist's threats to stay on SWAT—and if he finds out about Grant and Maggie's blossoming romance, FBI rules say one of them has to go.

Nikki Delacorte—Scott and Maggie's youngest sister. She still lives back in Indiana, but she wants to be there for Maggie as the anniversary approaches.

Chapter One

"Invisibility in three...two...one...now!"

The words echoed in Maggie Delacorte's earbud as her SWAT teammate stepped back from the neat hole he'd cut in the window. Behind her, everything was quiet in the predawn darkness. But that wouldn't last for long.

The FBI had gotten the word that a wanted fugitive was hiding out in this gang-infested part of DC, armed with an AK-47 and surrounded by a pack of die-hard supporters. Maggie and her teammates were here to make sure his time on the run was finished.

She moved quickly forward, tossing a flash-bang grenade through the window. The world in front of her exploded in white light, a massive *boom* echoing as the flash bang landed. Smoke billowed, providing cover.

"Go, go, go!" Grant Larkin yelled in that deep voice that always sent goose bumps running up her arms, as he used a ram and his massive upper-body strength to break down the door.

Maggie raced around the corner to follow, just as the door flew open into the one-story hideout. Grant went in first, moving right as planned, then the two teammates behind him dodged the splintered door and went left.

Her MP-5 raised and ready, Maggie barely felt the weight of the extra fifty pounds of gear she carried as she darted through the door, clearing it fast the way she'd been trained.

A bullet whizzed by her ear, coming from her left, but she didn't turn her head. That was in a teammate's sector. He'd handle the threat. Maggie's sector was straight ahead, and she stayed focused as she forged through the swirling gray smoke.

Reports came in over her radio as she entered the hallway to the bedrooms. The fugitive's allies were dwindling fast, either from bullets, or because they threw their hands up and their weapons down at the sight of the six FBI SWAT agents converging on them. But there were at least two left, including the fugitive himself, a three-time offender, who was surely looking at a life sentence this time around.

A gangbanger popped out of a doorway ahead of her, his modified AK-47 coming up fast, and Maggie moved her weapon right, firing at center mass.

The threat down, she kept going until she was beside Grant. He outweighed her by a solid eighty pounds and in the narrow hallway, with all their gear, they barely fit side by side.

He nodded his head to acknowledge her presence, glancing briefly her way. She registered it through her peripheral vision, but kept her focus where it needed to be: on the rooms to the right side. One more for her to clear, one for Grant.

Grant went through the doorway to the left and Maggie through the one on the right, her weapon instantly sighting on the threat in the corner. The fugitive himself, all three hundred pounds of him.

His finger quivered on the trigger, and Maggie barked, "Drop it! FBI!"

She'd been on the Washington Field Office's SWAT

team for the past four years, but perps sometimes made the mistake of thinking she wouldn't fire just because she was a woman. So Maggie leveled her meanest stare at him, hoping he could see it through her goggles. She wanted this guy alive, wanted him to rot in a cell and help them bring down the rest of his crew.

He scowled back at her with a nasty grimace even as his eyes watered from the smoke. But the modified AK-47 he'd been clutching fell to the floor beside him.

From the room across the hall, she could hear Grant yelling at another suspect to get down on the ground, and Maggie demanded the same of the fugitive.

She didn't get close until he'd followed her order to lie flat on his stomach on the filthy carpet, his hands clasped behind his head. Then she switched her MP-5 to safe mode, slung it over her back and unhooked the handcuffs from her belt. She approached him and planted a heavy knee in the center of his huge back. Yanking his left hand down fast, she slapped on the cuff then grabbed his right hand.

As she shifted her balance right, he ripped his cuffed hand away, using his bulk to toss her sideways.

She landed hard on her MP-5, and pain tore through her back. That was going to bruise. Cursing loud and creatively, she was up before he could get to his feet. Wrenching his cuffed arm backward, she rammed a foot in his armpit.

He squealed as she muttered under her breath about men who thought bigger meant they had the upper hand. A decade ago, she might have agreed with that assessment. But six years in the FBI, four of them on the super-competitive SWAT team, had taught her it just wasn't true.

She didn't have to be bigger. She just had to know how to leverage her strength, and her skill set.

The fugitive was still screeching as she slapped the cuff on his other wrist and then Grant was in the room, dragging a gangbanger behind him as if the guy weighed nothing. He took a handful of the fugitive's shirt, and the two of them pulled him to his feet.

"Nice job, Delacorte," Grant said.

Her heart rate—which had stayed relatively even during the entire arrest—picked up at the sound of his voice.

Grant Larkin had moved from the New York Field Office to the Washington Field Office, WFO, and her SWAT team, nine months ago. He was just shy of six feet, but even on a team filled with muscle-bound men, he stood out. The guy was *built*, which was why he was usually the door-kicker.

He also had deep brown eyes, light brown skin and an infectious grin, even in the middle of a grueling SWAT workout. In short, exactly her type. If only he wasn't a teammate, making him off-limits. And if only she didn't have baggage from her past that weighed more than he did.

Maggie nodded at him and called in their status over her radio. She got the "all clear" from all sectors and told Grant, "We're set. Let's get out of here."

"Sounds like a plan to me," he replied, letting her go ahead of him with the fugitive as he brought up the rear with the cuffed gangbanger.

The rest of the team was waiting outside the dilapidated one-story, loading a few other prisoners into their vehicle for transport. A couple of her teammates hooted when they saw her pushing the enormous, scowling fugitive in front of her.

She grinned back, because she knew they were laughing at the furious threats the fugitive was making, and not at the fact that she, at five foot eight and a hundred and forty pounds, was bringing him out. She'd worked with most of them for four years, and they'd learned fast not to coddle or underestimate her because she was a woman.

That was why being on SWAT had been good for her. It had shown her exactly how much she was capable of, and she wouldn't trade it for anything.

After they'd loaded the last two prisoners, Grant came over to her, yanking his goggles up over his helmet, and leaving behind indents around his eyes that didn't diminish his attractiveness at all. "I think this calls for celebration."

"O'Reilley's?" Clive Dekker, the team leader, asked. It was the pub the team usually hit after a particularly good or bad day.

It didn't matter that it was almost three in the morning. O'Reilley's catered to cops. They stopped serving liquor at two, but they were open twenty-four hours. And after the adrenaline rush of a high-risk arrest, most of the team couldn't just go home and go to sleep.

"Let's do it," Grant agreed. He turned to her, looking hopeful. "Delacorte?"

She hadn't gone with them in six months. Not since she'd started getting the letters, because the stress of it made it impossible to go out and joke around, to pretend everything was okay.

A lump filled her throat, and she tried to push back the memory that always surged forward when September 1 came around. In exactly thirty days, it would be ten years since the day that had changed her life. The day that had led her to the FBI. To SWAT.

And whatever happened on that tenth anniversary, would she regret not having spent as much time with Grant Larkin as she could?

She nodded at him. "Sure. I'm going to run home first. I'll meet you all there."

He looked surprised, but then grinned in a way that made her positive she'd made the right choice.

She stared back at him, momentarily rooted in place. Maybe it was time to forget her past. Maybe it was time to forget the rules.

Maybe it was time to see what could happen between her and Grant Larkin.

MAGGIE FELT HERSELF smiling with anticipation as she unlocked the bolts on her DC row house and entered, flipping on the lights. She stepped over the mail scattered in the entryway, realizing she hadn't been home in close to twenty-four hours.

As she locked the door behind her and kicked off her boots, it occurred to her that she should be exhausted. She'd worked a full day on her regular FBI civil rights squad, then been out with her brother and best friend when she'd gotten the call to come back for the SWAT arrest. But she was full of energy. When was the last time she'd been this happy?

Six months ago, she realized. Before the first letter had arrived. Grant had been on her team for three months at the time. They'd hit it off from his first day. Besides being a solid addition to the team, he was funny and just so dang happy all the time. Being around him made *her* happy.

SWAT was an ancillary position—agents did it on top of their regular squad duties. Still, dating a teammate, even in a secondary team like SWAT, was forbidden. So she'd tried to keep her feelings hidden. But just knowing that she was capable of feeling this way, after everything...

Stop dwelling on the past, Maggie scolded herself. She knew Grant had been able to tell these past few months that something was wrong. But unlike a lot of agents at the WFO, who'd heard the rumors over the years, she was pretty sure Grant didn't know her history. And she wanted to keep it that way.

She liked the way he looked at her, no trace of pity or worry. He'd never shown any sign that he'd heard about her past. The case agents had been good about keeping her connection under wraps over the years; though inevitably agents who'd been in DC for a long time found out. But Grant had only been here nine months. In that time, the only thing she'd ever seen in his eyes was friendship and camaraderie. And lately, something else, something that went beyond the bonds of the team.

Maggie carried her gear up the narrow stairs to her bedroom, flipping lights on along the way, then stared into her closet. She didn't own date clothes. Not that this was a date.

Everything in her closet belonged to a woman who, somewhere deep inside, was still afraid. Not of being a victim, not anymore. But when was the last time she'd actually wanted a man to look at her with appreciation?

Frowning, Maggie grabbed what she'd always worn to O'Reilley's—jeans, combat-style boots way too similar to the ones she wore for SWAT and a loose-fitting T-shirt. They'd only stay an hour or so anyway, chat and play darts and let the adrenaline fade. Then, one by one, the exhaustion would inevitably hit, and they'd head home and conk out.

She needed to get over there, or she'd miss everyone. Changing quickly, she looked into the bathroom mirror, taking a minute to lift her shirt up and look at the damage to her back. A bruise was blooming fast, huge and purple, snaking its way along her spine in the general shape of a sub-machine gun.

She poked at it and flinched, then pulled her shirt back down, combing a finger through her bob. It was just long enough to cover the back of her neck, and Maggie's fingers twitched as they skimmed the puckered skin there.

The tattoo she'd gotten years ago hid the image of a hook, but nothing could fix the damaged skin underneath. The brand that had been left on her.

She threw some water on her face, then dug through the drawer under her sink until she came up with some lipstick and mascara. The guys were probably going to stare at her as though she'd grown an extra head. Or maybe they wouldn't even notice. Most of them were like brothers.

Only Grant might spot—and appreciate—her pathetic attempt to look a little more feminine, since most of the time she tried to hide it.

She stared at herself in the mirror, resisting the urge to wipe off the makeup, then laughed aloud. She was being ridiculous. Just because she didn't wear makeup to work didn't mean everyone at the bar would know why she'd put it on tonight.

Maggie took the stairs down two at a time, still grinning. It wasn't that she didn't date, but most of the time, even when she truly had feelings for a guy, it felt obligatory. An attempt to feel normal that never quite worked.

But nothing about Grant Larkin felt obligatory.

And she was ready to take a chance. She had no idea how they'd handle the FBI rules—assuming he was interested. But the heated glances he hadn't quite been able to hide over the past few weeks told her he was.

At the bottom of the stairs, Maggie picked up the pile of mail and dumped it on the table and reached for her keys. But before she'd finished turning away, dread rushed over her. The plain business envelope. The corner of a neatly printed return label sticking out from the huge pile of mail like a flashing beacon.

She looked back at the mail slowly, dreading what she was going to find. But she hadn't been dreaming. She didn't have to open it to know. Another letter.

All the excitement drained out of her, buried under a decade-old fear.

Her movements robotic, she walked into her kitchen and slipped on a pair of latex gloves before returning to the front hall, even though she knew there'd be no prints. There never were.

She shouldn't even open it. It was evidence in an ongoing case. She should call the agents from the Violent Crimes Major Offenders, VCMO, squad assigned to the case. They'd have to be called anyway, because this letter would have to go in the case file along with the others. She should just let the case agents open it.

But even knowing what would be inside, she couldn't stop herself from carefully slicing open the top of the envelope. She slid out the plain white paper and unfolded it carefully, only touching the edges. She knew it was useless, but she still tried to numb herself as she started reading.

Anger and resentment—along with the guilt and shame she couldn't suppress—crept forward, even as she tried to remain clinical and approach it the way she would one of her own cases. It read just like the previous letters, three of them over the past six months. To someone who didn't know the sender, it would sound like a love letter, fondly recalling their time together.

But it wasn't. It was a letter from the Fishhook Rapist, the predator who'd evaded capture for almost a decade.

The predator who had started by abducting her on her way home to her dorm room at George Washington University all those years ago. He'd let her go the next morning, drugged and disoriented, carrying a permanent reminder on the back of her neck.

Maggie felt herself sway and clutched the table as she read the last line. It was different from any of the previous letters.

The Fishhook Rapist was coming back to DC. And he was coming back for her.

Chapter Two

"You got another one?" Maggie's older brother, Scott, was scowling furiously, clenching his fists so tightly, the knuckles looked ready to break through skin. He was standing in the entryway to her row house a mere thirty minutes after she'd called him, which meant he'd broken a lot of traffic laws to get there.

Normally, Scott was all charm, all the time, with an easy grin and a swagger. But today, even with his eyes red from being ripped from sleep before dawn, he looked angrier than she'd seen him in a long, long time.

Their best friend, Ella Cortez, had arrived ten minutes earlier; she lived within DC and closer to Maggie's house. Maggie had called them instead of heading to the bar, and Ella had gotten in her car practically before Maggie had finished telling her what had happened.

Now Ella put a hand on Scott's arm and gave him a look Maggie could read as well as Scott could. *Go easy.*

The three of them had grown up together, back in Buckley, Indiana, and Ella might as well have been her and Scott's other sister. After Maggie's assault her senior year of college, they'd made a pact together. Throw out all their plans for the future and join the FBI. Stop this kind of thing from happening to anyone else.

But she couldn't even stop the man who'd hurt her.

Maggie tightened her jaw, tried not to let them see her fear. "Yes. But the letter was different this time. He said he's coming back to DC. He said he's coming back for me."

"What?" Scott shouted.

He ran a hand through his close-cut blond hair, and she could see him trying to rein in his fury.

Scott was a year older than she was. They'd always been close, but since her attack, he'd become even more protective. She'd expected him to worry less once she'd joined SWAT, but it was only recently that his new girlfriend had taught him to loosen up at all. That would change back now.

"Have the case agents taken the letter?" Scott asked. As a sniper with the FBI's Hostage Rescue Team, Scott was used to being able to take action. Not knowing who the threat was drove him crazy.

"Were those his exact words? That he was coming back to DC, coming back for you?" Ella asked. She was calmer, but Maggie still heard her worry.

"They just picked it up," she told Scott, then looked at Ella. "His exact words were, 'I'm coming home for our anniversary.'" She choked the words out. Even saying them made bile rise up in her throat.

Scott swore, and Ella paled, but she still nodded thoughtfully. "Home," Ella mused.

Her brother took a loud, calming breath, but rage still filled his eyes. "What do you think it means?"

Just like her, Scott had gravitated toward a specialty that would let him physically, personally, take down threats. On the outside, they didn't resemble each other at all, though they were only a year apart in age. Scott was a head taller than her at six feet, with blond hair and chocolate-brown eyes. She looked more like their younger sister, Nikki, with her dark brown hair and light blue eyes.

But inside, they were so similar, both of them attacking every challenge head-on.

Ella was different. She'd been the glue that had held them together, kept them from butting heads over the years. And while Scott and Maggie had gone into physical specialties with the FBI, Ella had wanted to understand. So she'd become a profiler with the Behavioral Analysis Unit. If there was anyone who had a chance of deciphering the Fishhook Rapist's motivations—and hopefully his next move—it would be her.

"What does it mean?" Ella repeated. "Well, it could be the obvious."

"That he was born here," Scott replied, nodding. "Okay. What else?"

"Well, we know he doesn't live here now."

Part of the reason the Fishhook Rapist had managed to evade capture for so long was because he moved around a lot. He claimed one victim a year, and never in the same place. His last victim had been in Florida, and the second letter Maggie had gotten had been postmarked from there.

The first one had come from Georgia, and the most recent one had originated in North Carolina.

"Then, what?" Scott demanded.

Ella frowned, her deep brown eyes pensive. "This guy is a narcissist. He brags about what he does. It's why he lets his victims go. He wants the attention, and he gets off on knowing the women he abducts can't identify him. His attacks have become the main source of pride in his life. So the location of his first attack—"

"You think he might see DC as home because it's where he assaulted me," Maggie broke in.

She'd gone to school here—and she'd even finished out her senior year after her attack, putting all her focus into her new goal of making it to the FBI—but then she'd moved back to her parents' house in Indiana for a while, wanting to put physical distance between her and the memories. When she'd made it through the FBI Academy, and they'd assigned her to the DC office, she'd almost backed out.

But she'd stuck with it, then worked her way onto the SWAT team. DC had truly become her home now. It made her sick that he thought of it as his, too.

Ella looked uncomfortable, but she didn't fidget or honey-coat anything. "Yes. It's the start of where he got his name."

The media had dubbed him the Fishhook Rapist after they'd gotten wind of what he did to his victims, branding them on the backs of their necks with the image of a hook. Maggie's hand tensed with the need to touch the puckered skin on her neck that would never be smooth, but she clutched her hands together.

Ella looked apologetic as she finished, "To him, this is home."

Nausea welled up, and Maggie sank onto her couch. Scott sat next to her, wrapping an arm around her shoulder. A few seconds later, Ella was on her other side, hooking their arms together.

"He can write as many letters as he wants, but he's not getting anywhere near you," Scott vowed, in the dark, determined tone he probably used on the job. It sounded convincing.

So did Ella when she added, "We're going to get him, Maggie. He's making a mistake trying to come back here."

She wanted to believe it. Wanted to believe that the

case agents, and her brother and Ella and all of her FBI and SWAT training were enough to keep her safe.

But that fear she'd pushed down for ten years rose up, strong and painful, like the feel of fiery metal on the back of her neck.

Maggie squeezed her eyes closed, grasping her brother and Ella by the arms. "I'm not supposed to be anywhere near the case."

"Doesn't matter," Ella said. She was a stickler for doing everything by the book—except when it came to a possible lead on this particular case.

"We're not waiting for that SOB to come after you," Scott agreed. "And we're not leaving this to the case agents, no matter how good they are."

Maggie nodded, tears welling up in her eyes at their loyalty. "It's time to go on the offensive."

WHERE WAS SHE?

Grant Larkin tried not to stare through the near-empty pub at the entrance to O'Reilley's, but he couldn't stop himself, the same way he couldn't stop himself from taking a peek at his watch. The team had been at the pub for a solid two hours, letting the adrenaline from the arrest fade.

Now daylight was rapidly approaching. Even though it was Saturday, and they got a break, a couple of them were heading out the door, along with the last of the cops who'd been in the pub when they'd arrived.

Maggie wasn't coming.

"What happened to Delacorte?" Clive Dekker asked, looking at Grant as if he would know.

Grant shrugged, but he'd been resisting the urge to call her for the past hour and find out. He'd been shocked when she'd agreed to join them, after six months of skipping out on anything social. Even more shocked by the way she'd looked at him while agreeing. As if she was as interested in him as he was in her.

He'd been drawn to her from the moment they'd met, nine months ago. For most of that time, he'd tried to keep his attraction hidden. They were teammates, a definite Bureau no-no. Lately, though, he hadn't been able to suppress it, and he knew she'd noticed. But she'd never looked at him quite the way she had tonight, as if maybe she wanted more from him. If only...

"Well, I'm calling it, before my wife sends out a search party," Clive said, then squinted, leaning closer to him in the noisy pub. "Is that your phone ringing?"

Grant grinned at him. "I think you're still hearing the aftereffects of that flash bang, old man," he joked. The team leader was thirty-nine, only four years older than Grant. But Clive was the oldest guy on the Washington Field Office SWAT team.

"Ha ha," Clive replied. "It's *your* hearing that's going." He slapped Grant on the shoulder as he maneuvered out of the booth. "That was definitely your phone."

Grant frowned and took out his FBI-issued Black-Berry. Clive was right. One missed call. Hoping it was Maggie saying she was on her way, he held in a yawn and dialed his voice mail.

The message was from the supervisor of his Violent Crimes Major Offenders, VCMO, squad. SWAT was his calling, but VCMO was his regular position at the FBI, the job that filled most of his days.

"We've got a situation," the supervisory special agent said in his typical no-nonsense way. "I need you back at the field office, ASAP."

That was the extent of the message. Grant swore as he slapped some money on the table to cover his drink, then told his remaining teammates, "Gotta go. I'll catch you guys on Monday."

"Hot date?" one of them asked.

"I wish," Grant said. And boy, did he. If only Maggie had shown tonight. "But that was my SSA. Duty calls."

It was a short drive back to the office, which was oddly busy for 5:00 a.m. on a Saturday morning. Not that this was a nine-to-five sort of job, but from the amount of agents gathered in one of the interagency conference rooms, something big had broken. Or they wanted it to.

It wasn't *his* VCMO squad in the conference room, so Grant strode past with only a curious glance inside. His own SSA was waiting in the drab gray bullpen, a scowl on his face as he marked up a stack of paperwork.

"Thanks for coming in," James said, not glancing up as he wrote frantic notes on whatever case file he was reviewing.

Judging from the way his rapidly receding gray hair was sticking out, and the heavier-than-usual shadows under his eyes, the SSA had never left yesterday. But that was pretty standard for James.

"What's happening?" Grant asked, wishing he'd stopped for a coffee instead of settling for the bitter junk they brewed in the office. He'd been up nearly twenty-four hours straight now, and he was heading for a crash that even caffeine could only hold off for so long.

"Hang on." James finished whatever he was writing, then pushed it aside and looked up at Grant, a deep frown on his face.

Discomfort wormed through Grant. In his gut, he knew that whatever was happening, he *really* wasn't going to like it. "What is it?"

James sighed and rubbed a hand over his craggy face. With three divorces under his belt, he was now just married to the job. He was a tough supervisor, and he rarely looked stressed. But right now he looked very, very stressed. "Take a seat. Let's chat."

Grant tugged a chair over and sat down. "Spit it out."

James smiled, probably because Grant was one of the few agents in his VCMO squad who would push him. But the smile faded fast. "You know the situation with the Fishhook Rapist case, right?"

Grant cursed. Everyone who worked violent crime knew the background on that case. A sadistic rapist who grabbed one woman a year off the street, drugged, raped and branded her, then let her go, too disoriented to provide a description of her attacker. There was never any useful forensic evidence.

The guy was way too smart. He surfaced only on September 1, when a new victim would show up at a police station or hospital somewhere in the country, branded with his signature. Then he disappeared again, until the following year, when he'd hit some other state and leave a new victim.

And he'd started with Maggie Delacorte.

That part wasn't general knowledge—they didn't advertise the names of the victims, and they tried to keep the press from getting too much information. They inevitably did, but somehow, the FBI had managed to keep Maggie's last name out of the media for a decade, along with the fact that she'd moved on to become a standout SWAT agent.

Inside the Bureau, however, a few rumors had gotten out over the years, and when he'd moved to WFO and landed on her SWAT team, he'd heard the whispers.

She worked harder than just about anyone he knew, and he was positive she didn't want one terrible incident in her past to color the way her colleagues looked at her, so he'd never said anything. To him, it didn't change a thing. Not about what he thought of her work, and definitely not about how he felt about her as a woman.

"Grant!" his boss snapped, and he realized he hadn't been paying attention.

"Sorry." He ran a hand over his shaved head, dreading whatever he was about to hear. They had a month to go before the guy was supposed to surface, so any news about him now could in theory be a lead to catch him. But judging by his boss's face, Grant didn't think that was it.

"I said, is this going to be a problem for you?"

"What?"

James let out a heavy sigh. "You know about the letters, right?"

"Letters?" Grant frowned and shook his head.

"The perp's been sending them to Maggie over the last six months."

Anger boiled inside. No wonder Maggie hadn't been herself lately.

Did anyone on the team know? He felt his frown deepening, certain she wouldn't have told any of them, no matter how close the team was.

"The case agents checked with the other victims," James continued. "None of the others have received anything. But Maggie got a new one last night." He looked at his watch. "This morning, actually."

Grant looked toward the bustling conference room. So that was why the other VCMO squad had gathered. Maggie must have found the letter when she'd gone home. Which explained why she'd never shown at the bar.

Now he really wished he'd called her, even though chances were, she wouldn't have asked for his help.

"This letter was different from the others. The others were psychological-sick, but meant to hurt from a distance. This one was a threat. And given *your* background…" James stared expectantly at him, not needing to finish his sentence.

Grant had worked in the New York field office for eight years before moving to WFO, and while he'd been there, he'd closed a serial murder case with unusual elements. Specific dates of attacks over a number of years, letters to one particular victim. In that case, it was a woman who had escaped.

"You think my experience on the Manhattan Strangler case—"

"Could help close this one," James finished. "Yes. Kammy Ming has requested you be moved to her squad for the duration of the case. Full-time. We're going to catch him before the next anniversary. There's no other option."

"He said he was coming back for Maggie, didn't he?" Grant asked, shades of the homicide case he'd closed coming back to him. The warm blood spurting on him as he'd driven the perp's knife into him. Carrying the victim out to the ambulance, then being shoved in with her to have his own wounds stitched up.

Grant had caught the guy four years after he'd started killing, but it had almost been too late for the woman he'd come back for. The thought of Maggie being loaded into an ambulance made him queasy.

"Look, Kammy wants your help," James said. "But if you being on SWAT with Maggie is going to be a conflict…"

Suddenly glad he was sitting down, Grant shook his head and hoped for once, James's intuition would fail him.

"Are you sure?" James persisted. "Because once she hears you're on the case, if she asks you about it, you still have to keep it all confidential. Can you do that?"

Could he? He wasn't sure. Worse yet, Grant was pretty sure Maggie had no idea he knew about her past. How would she react to him being on the case now?

Did he even want to be on this case? He didn't have to ask Maggie to know she wouldn't want him involved.

It was one thing to walk into dangerous situations with her—he trained with her and knew she could handle herself. But to go through all the details of what had happened to her a decade ago, back when she'd been a scared college kid? Being her friend now, feeling the way he did about her, did he have any right to dig into the worst day of her life, without her permission?

"Well?" James demanded, staring expectantly.

Then again, how could he sit by and not do anything when he had a chance to stop the man who'd hurt her?

Rage and determination filled him in equal measure, drowning out the nausea. "Yes, I want in on the investigation."

"Good," James said, standing up. "Then, get in the conference room. You start right now."

Chapter Three

"Why now?" Maggie asked as she walked into her living room. "And how long have you been up?" she added, noticing the pillows and blankets she'd put on the couch for Scott looked untouched. The guest room bed she'd made up for Ella was probably still made, too.

She glanced at her watch—10:00 a.m. Which meant she'd been in bed for about four hours. Not that she'd slept much. She'd spent most of the time trying every combat nap technique she'd learned from Scott, who'd trained with military special operations teams for his HRT sniper position. Still, every time she'd drifted off to sleep, she'd startled awake almost immediately.

Despite having gotten out of bed at five in the morning when she'd called them over, Ella and Scott looked wide-awake.

Ella handed her a cup of coffee. "We stayed up."

"What did I miss?" Maggie asked, looking back and forth between them. But neither of them needed to answer. She could tell from their faces. "You talked about how you were going to protect me, didn't you?"

"Don't be ridiculous," Scott said. "We both know you can take care of yourself."

"Thank—"

"But that doesn't mean we're leaving you alone," he

cut her off, putting a hand on her arm. "Get ready for some houseguests. Or pack a bag. And don't even think about arguing."

Maggie was both annoyed and relieved. If it was one of them in trouble, she'd be doing the same thing. They were a team; they always had been.

"Okay. But I want to stay here." They could take turns staying with her—she knew there was no stopping them—but she didn't want to bring trouble to their doorsteps.

Especially since neither one lived alone. Ella's fiancé, Logan, was a cop, and Scott's girlfriend, Chelsie—who'd moved in with him a week ago—was FBI. But neither of them had signed up for this, and although Maggie knew they'd help if she asked, she didn't want to drag them into it, too.

Scott looked surprised at her easy agreement, but he changed the subject, probably worried she'd change her mind. "Maggie, you haven't told Mom and Dad about the letters, have you? Or Nikki?"

"No." She took a sip of coffee, and the hot liquid burned the back of her throat, clearing her head. "And I don't plan to now, either. What are they going to do from Indiana, besides worry?"

She got ready to fight Scott on it—her parents had worried enough about her, ten years ago. She didn't want them repeating it now. And Nikki had only been twelve then, so they'd tried to keep the details from her. Nikki knew now—since the Fishhook Rapist had never been caught, she'd read about him in the news over the years. But Maggie didn't want her little sister to worry, especially not while Nikki was just moving into her first apartment, starting her first job.

"I agree," Scott said, surprising her.

"You do?"

"Yes. We both know Mom and Dad will just call you constantly, insisting you come home. And you don't need the distraction. We need to focus on stopping him. I want this September 1 to be just another day."

So did she. Getting together with Ella and Scott once a year, praying a new victim wouldn't turn up, was a tradition she'd love to forsake. But September 1 was never going to be just another day for her.

"Good," she said. "Then let's get started."

"You don't have access to the case file, do you?" Ella asked.

Maggie snorted. "No." She knew more details than the average victim, because the task force had asked her questions over the years. But they'd never let her officially investigate. She suppressed a shudder at just the idea. Even if it could help, the thought of looking through all the other victim files—and her own—made the coffee churn in her stomach.

"It probably wouldn't tell us a lot more than we already know, anyway."

She didn't have to say why. The news gave them enough details about where the Fishhook Rapist had been, and it was no secret he'd stuck to a pattern. Victimology and the crime itself hadn't changed.

He always struck once a year, on the same date. And he always chose the same type of woman: someone in her late teens or early twenties, with a slender build and long, dark hair.

Maggie touched the hair she'd cut into a bob years ago, after the second Fishhook Rapist victim had surfaced, looking too much like her. She'd worked hard on her physique, too. No longer was she thin and willowy, but lean and muscular.

She turned her back on Scott and Ella, in the pretense of heading for the chair in the corner, but really to give herself a second without being scrutinized to get her game face on. The face she used when she went into a SWAT call and needed a perp who weighed more than twice as much as she did to recognize her as a viable threat. She could do this. She could talk about what had happened to her, with the two people closest to her in the world.

Her bruised back protested as she sat. When she raised her eyes to theirs, she could tell Ella and Scott weren't fooled. In some ways, this would be easier with total strangers.

Clutching the arms of her chair too hard, she asked Ella, "Why now? Why isn't this year the same as every other one? Do you think he plans to target a new victim, too? Or just come back for me? And what—" She choked on the rest of the sentence, but she could tell Ella knew what she was going to ask.

What did he plan to do to her this time?

Ella settled onto the couch across from her, her face scrunched up, and Maggie knew what was coming. A detailed profiler's analysis.

Ella looked pensive as she started, "It was a sophisticated crime. He didn't leave us any forensic evidence, not even the first time. He was probably in his late twenties a decade ago. Young enough to fit in around a college town, but old enough to be self-sufficient, with his own vehicle and the ability to leave town permanently afterward without attracting attention."

Scott was nodding from his perch next to the couch as Ella continued, "He's closing in on forty now, and he's still grabbing women in college or just out of it. It's not as easy for him to blend in anymore. He's starting to realize he needs to think about changing his approach. He's starting to realize his pattern for the past decade has to change, at least in some ways. It's made him reminisce. And ten years is a significant number, in terms of standard anniversaries."

Intense lines appeared on Ella's smooth olive skin, and even her tone changed as she got into what Maggie recognized as her profiler groove. "To this perp, September 1 is more important than any standard anniversary. He's not married, never has been, and for him, this crime dominates his life."

She looked apologetic as she continued, "You're important to him because that day was the start for him. It probably wasn't his first offense, but it was the first time he used the brand." Her voice caught as she said, "And that's his signature. As he's been planning his next attack, he can't stop thinking about how it all started. He's looking for that same thrill, the way it was the first time he decided to act—the fear and excitement and—"

Ella closed her eyes again, and Maggie realized this was as hard for Ella to profile as it was for Maggie to hear. Ella had been there that day, when Maggie had stumbled back to their dorm room, drugged and only able to remember fragments of what had happened. Fragments were all she had today, and in some ways, she was grateful for that.

Scott was standing beside the couch, his jaw locked, his nostrils practically flaring, as he listened silently.

Maggie got up and walked woodenly to the couch, sitting beside Ella, who'd befriended her and Scott when she'd moved down the street from them when she and Maggie were in kindergarten. "It's okay. Keep going."

Maggie could hear determination, sorrow and anger in Ella's voice as she said, "It's hard for me to profile him objectively, Maggie. But I don't think he's planning to go after a new victim this year. I think he means what he says in that letter. I think he's coming back here just for you, to re-create what's in his mind from a decade ago."

"THE DATE OF the attacks has to mean something," Grant announced Monday morning.

He'd been saying it for two days now, and he was certain he was right. The problem was, he didn't know what it meant.

"Maybe." Kammy Ming, the SSA of the VCMO squad where Grant was on loan, still looked skeptical.

They were the only ones in the room now, but in an hour, it would fill up with the rest of the case agents. Kammy was already here because, as far as he could tell, she didn't sleep. He was here extra early because he needed to figure this out, for Maggie.

"Or maybe it's just the day he went after what he wanted," Kammy said. "Maybe it's important *because* it's the date of the attacks. Because it's when he abducted Maggie, so then it became his day for every future attack."

"Yeah, I know that's the prevailing theory," Grant said, rolling his shoulders, which were tight from spending the weekend sitting in an uncomfortable chair in a WFO conference room. "But you wanted me here because of my experience with the Manhattan Strangler case, right?"

Kammy nodded, but she was frowning, looking exhausted after a weekend without much progress. "There are some compelling similarities we can't ignore. But this isn't the same guy…"

"No," Grant agreed. "But in that case, the killer specifically waited for the anniversary of his mother's death to make a kill. Four years, and he was in control enough to wait a whole year in between attacks. With someone who has this sort of compulsion, a year is a long wait."

"Keep talking," Kammy said, tying her graying hair up in a bun as she stared expectantly at him.

She was as much of a workaholic as James. Was that going to be him in ten years? No balance, just the job all the time?

An image of Maggie immediately filled his brain. There was a heck of a lot more than work that he wanted to fill his days. And there was a heck of a lot more than just work involved when it came to solving this case.

"It's the same with this guy," Grant pressed. "He's systematic with the abductions, the branding, every single year. But he can control the urge until September 1 comes along. There must be a reason."

Kammy raised her eyebrows, sinking back into the chair next to him. "You have any ideas *why* the Fishhook Rapist would choose that specific day every year?" Before he could answer, she added, "Why did the Manhattan Strangler wait for the anniversary of his mother's death every year?"

"He was textbook. Overbearing mother he hated. He'd threatened to kill her for years, but could never bring himself to do it. After she died in a car accident, he treated the new victims as surrogates. So he waited for her anniversary for each kill."

Kammy nodded thoughtfully. "Trying to kill his mother over and over again, in the form of women who resembled her."

"Exactly. And the Fishhook Rapist chooses victims with a definite look, so it's possible he's modeling them after someone, too, but it could just be that he has a type. And given the rape, I think his motivation is different."

"Such as?"

It was 6:00 a.m. Monday morning, and they'd been going over the evidence practically nonstop since he'd been called in early Saturday. He was exhausted. But he didn't think he'd be able to sleep even if he wanted to. Every time he closed his eyes, he thought of the case. He thought of Maggie's case file.

He thought of Maggie, the way he knew her now. Light blue eyes bright with intelligence and determination, dark brown hair framing her heart-shaped face, lean body outlined with muscle, primed to rush into a SWAT call. And he thought of her the way he'd seen her in the photographs from her case file, taken at the hospital shortly after her attack. Smaller and much younger, hunched into herself, battered and broken. He never wanted to see her like that again.

Straightening, he shook his head. "I don't know. Maybe we should talk to a profiler—"

Kammy cut him off. "This case has been to the BAU. One of their senior people profiled him for us a few years ago."

"Okay, so what'd they say about the date of the attacks?"

"He said there wasn't enough evidence to be sure either way."

"But if we could figure out what it was, maybe it would help us track him."

Kammy nodded. "Well, you have any ideas, then go for it. In the meantime, let's work with what we know. Why's he coming back for Maggie?"

"Because he couldn't claim her," Grant replied immediately. To him, that one was obvious.

It had been the same with the Manhattan Strangler. He'd come back for the one woman who'd escaped him, the one woman he'd tried to kill who had managed to survive, against all the doctors' predictions.

Kammy's eyebrows drew together. "He *did* claim her. He raped and branded her like the rest—"

"Yeah, but look at her now." Grant cut Kammy off, not wanting or needing the reminder of what Maggie had endured. "She's SWAT. She didn't let him break her. And she was the first one he went after, the one with the most meaning to him."

"You think he knew her personally?"

"Probably not, but I think he watched her from afar for a while. I think there's a good chance he had a legitimate reason to be at the college back then."

"You mean a student?" Kammy shook her head. "The profiler was pretty solid on the guy being older than his victims."

"Maybe he worked there."

"Okay," Kammy said, "We can double-check. But they definitely looked closely at college employees back then. And I'm pretty sure we checked into anyone who moved after that attack, because we know he must have left between then and the following year, when he showed up in Mississippi. But let's go back to what you said about Maggie being different from the others."

Grant spun his chair back toward the conference table and took out eight of the nine victim files, handing them to Kammy. "The other victims. Look at their updates, the follow-ups. Look at where they are now. Every single one of them was derailed by the attack in some way. Either they dropped out of school, so they didn't end up in their planned profession, or they developed other problems like drinking or substance abuse."

Kammy started opening the files. "Okay, you're right about some of them. Two dropped out of school and never went back, which—you're right—seriously impacted their futures. One has a drinking problem and another one has had substance abuse issues, but she's clean now. Still, what about Marjorie? She—"

"Was on suicide watch on and off for two years after her attack."

"Danielle—"

"Dropped out of school, too."

"She's a doctor now," Kammy argued.

"She eventually went back to school. But it set her back about four years. And she's been vocal about her experience since then, including her struggle with panic attacks to this day."

Kammy stared at him. "This isn't all in the files."

"I did some digging. I know Maggie was his first victim, and ten years is an anniversary. But I think it's more than that. Maggie didn't just survive. She went into one of the most physical jobs in the FBI. Looking at her now, you'd never think she endured that. I think he's developed a sick obsession with her, with the idea of her and how he tried to leave a mark on her—psychologically, that is—and ultimately failed. I think he's coming back for her because he wants to break her."

Kammy snorted. "I know Maggie Delacorte, too, Grant. She's one of the toughest agents here. If he couldn't break her when she was twenty-two, how's he going to do it now, when she's SWAT?"

Grant shook his head, frowning. "I don't know." Which worried him a lot. Because the Fishhook Rapist was extremely intelligent. He had to be, to evade them for this many years, with this much Bureau heat on him. So he would have a plan in place.

Yet, he'd advertised that he was going to return for Maggie. He'd never returned for any of his victims. So they would never have expected it if he hadn't told them. Why would he do that? Unless it was part of his effort to break Maggie down.

"Well, whatever his plan is, we need to get to him before he gets near her. I don't care if she can take him down with her bare hands, I don't like this," Kammy said. "I don't like anything about this."

"Neither do I."

"We've got twenty-seven days," Kammy said. "And so far, zero leads."

"Then we'd better get cracking," Grant said, standing. "I'll get the number for the DC cops who handled the original case."

"Just remember," Kammy called after him, "You run into Maggie, and you say nothing."

"Not a problem," Grant said. He hoped she wouldn't discover that he was working the case until it was over. Until they'd put the Fishhook Rapist behind bars for good.

PEOPLE WERE STARING.

Maggie felt uncomfortable as she walked down the drab gray hallway toward the bustling bullpen where she worked at the WFO. Other agents avoided her eyes as she approached, but she could see them watching from her peripheral vision. As if they all knew.

The case agents for the Fishhook Rapist investigation worked out of the WFO, and it had been that way for a long time, so inevitably some rumors had gotten out. But never like this.

She jumped as someone clapped a hand on her shoulder, then spun around to face the office newbie, a tall, reed-thin guy a few months out of the Academy. Still all nervous excitement and no experience. Still too green to know when to keep his mouth shut.

He gave her an uncomfortable smile and said, "I can't believe the jerk is writing you letters. But they'll catch him. Don't worry."

Mind your own business formed on her lips, but she held it in and nodded stiffly back. Until now, only the longtime agents had seemed to know anything about what had led her into the FBI, and by the time they found out, they knew her well enough not to judge her for it. Six years at the WFO, and she'd never felt as though there was an invisible cloud of pity around her no one wanted to enter. It was why she'd almost backed out when the FBI had assigned her here in the first place.

Frustration and dismay filled her, and she gritted her teeth and tried to bury those emotions under anger. After ten years, the Fishhook Rapist shouldn't have this kind of power over her life anymore.

She wasn't going to *let* him have this kind of power over her life anymore.

She straightened her shoulders, and the newbie must have seen something in her eyes, because he stammered nervously about getting to work and hurried off.

"Maggie."

She turned at the sound of the familiar voice, and found Clive standing behind her, a grim expression on his normally friendly face.

"You know," she said, and her voice sounded weak and emotional. She cleared her throat and added, "Does everyone know?"

Did Grant know?

Clive's lips twisted with sympathy. "No, not everyone. But those of us who came in early today heard the case agents working. They had the conference room open, and they were going over the new evidence." He lowered his voice. "This is the first I've heard about the letters. I wish you'd said something, Maggie."

She shrugged, trying not to feel she'd somehow let him down. She knew he was aware of her history, because it had come up when she'd joined his team. But he'd made it clear then that her past didn't matter to him so long as it didn't affect her ability to do the job. And she'd proven, for four years now, that it didn't. "It wasn't relevant. It didn't affect my position in SWAT."

He gave her a small smile. "No, it didn't." The smile faded. "But with everything going on—"

Maggie put her hands on her hips. "You're pulling me from the team?"

"No. But I want you to think about whether it's the best place for you right now. If you want time—"

"I don't." She tried to force confidence into her tone and her expression. "The letters just mean there's more evidence to investigate. They won't affect my performance on the team."

Clive frowned, as if he could see through her. "We've been friends a long time, Maggie. I'm here if you want to talk. And if you need a break, we'll hold your spot. Don't worry about that."

"Okay." She nodded, a lump filling her throat. There were three SWAT teams at the Washington Field Office, and agents tended to stay on the teams for years—positions very rarely opened up, and waiting lists for tryouts were long. Clive offering to hold her spot was a huge commitment.

She needed to remember she had good friends here, and focus on that, instead of the unwanted attention she was getting right now from agents who barely knew her. "Thanks."

"Of course." He gave her a smile that looked a little

forced then headed for his own desk across the room, in the Organized Crime squad.

As he walked away, Maggie surveyed the other agents in the room. It hadn't been her imagination. There was definitely staring.

She dropped her bag at her desk, slid her gun and cuffs into her drawer and headed back down the hall toward the coffeepot.

Hopefully, Clive was right and only the agents who'd come in early today had learned about the letters. And hopefully, those agents would get over it, stop staring and not gossip.

But the thing she hoped for most was that Grant hadn't heard.

She had to believe the Bureau would catch the Fishhook Rapist this time. Before September 1. She refused to think anything else, no matter how dread filled her every time she thought about that date. No matter how the voice in the back of her mind sounded too much like a whisper from a decade ago, telling her, "This is going to hurt."

She had to believe it would all be over soon, and once it was, she wasn't going to let a few bureaucratic rules keep her from taking a chance with Grant Larkin. Assuming he wanted to take a chance with her. Assuming he hadn't learned all of her horrible secrets.

Please, please, don't let him know.

She chanted the words in her head as she reached the coffeepot. As she grabbed the carafe, Kammy Ming strode over, managing to project power despite her tiny five-foot frame.

"Maggie." Kammy greeted her in the subdued tone she seemed to save just for Maggie.

"Hi, Kammy," Maggie replied. "How's the case going?" She clutched the carafe too tightly, certain

Kammy wouldn't tell her anything. Kammy never told her anything.

But this time, Kammy carefully tugged the carafe from her hand, poured her a cup and said, "We worked all weekend. We're going to catch him."

A smile trembled on Maggie's lips as Kammy poured herself a cup, then faded as Kammy turned to leave, calling after her, "Your friend Grant has some good insights."

Grant was *on the case*? Dizziness washed over her, and she would have dropped her mug of hot coffee except a pair of large hands grabbed it and steadied her.

She looked up, and there was Grant, staring down at her with concern and guilt in his deep brown eyes.

He knew. He knew all the horrible details of what had happened to her. It may have been years ago, but that didn't change how men reacted when they found out. Especially men she was dating. Or wanted to date.

She stepped out of his grasp and braced herself.

"I'm sorry, Maggie," Grant whispered.

And right then and there, she knew anything that could have happened between them was over.

Chapter Four

"Get out of here."

"What?" Grant stopped rubbing his eyes and looked up at Kammy.

She was so tiny, she barely had height on him when she was standing, and he was sitting, but she glared like a pro. "You're no good to me if you're so exhausted you can't focus. Go home. Get some sleep. You've been here too long. Come back fresh tomorrow."

Grant started to argue, but Kammy reached for the file in front of him and closed it. Knowing she'd fight him if he tried to stay, he held up his hands in surrender and got to his feet.

As he trudged through the practically empty bullpen and into the equally deserted parking garage, he admitted she was right. He did need to recharge. Pure determination wasn't going to solve a case that had eluded dozens of other case agents and local police over the past decade. He needed to be at the top of his game, and to do that, a solid eight hours of sleep was in his immediate future.

He was already pressing the button to open his doors when he realized someone was sitting on the hood of his car.

Maggie stood as he approached, a familiar "don't mess

with me" glint in those pretty blue eyes, though she usually saved it for the dirtbags they arrested.

He hadn't asked her before agreeing to work on the case. That made him uncomfortable, but the fact was, even if she'd said she didn't want him on it, he couldn't have turned it down. Couldn't have sat by knowing he might have made a difference when the Fishhook Rapist was after Maggie again.

Grant rubbed the back of his neck and prepared for a fight. "You could have called me if you wanted to talk, Maggie. I would have come out."

She shook her head. "I wanted to do this without causing more gossip."

He cut her off before she could get going. "I should have told you. But I wanted to help."

"And you didn't think I'd prefer someone else work this case?" she said, straightforward as always. "We work some heavy calls together. Every time we clear a room now, are you going to think I can't handle it?"

"Of course no—" he started.

"Do you know how hard it is to be in this field office?" Strain filled her voice. "Knowing there's a squad full of agents who've read all about the worst day of my life?"

"I'm sorry." He'd thought about the strength it took to get through that, and the character it took to ignore the rumors. But he'd never thought about how she felt as a federal agent who investigated crimes all day long, to be part of a case file as a victim.

Probably because, even with what she'd gone through, he'd never thought of her as one. He'd always thought of her as a survivor.

"And do you know how much worse it is, knowing you've seen the evidence from my assault?" she whispered.

The information from her rape kit. It'd been one of the

hardest things he'd ever done, reading through it. And he'd read plenty of them over the years.

"They wanted my help," he said, trying to be honest with her. "It doesn't change a thing between us."

"You're wrong about that."

He stepped closer, reached out and lifted her hand, threading his fingers through hers. "I hope not." He stared into her eyes, trying to tell her with just his gaze how he felt.

Considering how surprised she seemed, it might even have worked.

But then she looked down at their locked hands and frowned. "I'm sure you'd love to think it doesn't make a difference, that it doesn't change how you view me. But believe me, it always does."

He tugged on her hand, bringing her closer, and forcing her to look up at him. "How many people have seen the case file?"

She shook her head. "*Knowing* what happened to me always changes how people look at me."

"I don't believe that." And he didn't. Everyone working the case had the highest respect for her.

He could tell she was about to argue, so he cut her off. "Maggie, I've known since I moved to the WFO."

Her jaw went slack, and her eyes widened. "What?"

"I work the violent crimes squads, and those squads share theories. Just because I wasn't on the case…" He shrugged. "I already knew."

"Why didn't you say anything?"

"Why would I say anything? You heard about me getting stabbed in the Manhattan Strangler case a few years back, right?"

She nodded, studying him as though she was trying to figure out whether or not to believe him.

"You never said anything about that."

"It's a little different."

"It's a lot different, I know. But just because something really bad happened to you a decade ago, that doesn't have anything to do with how I feel about you now."

He tugged her even closer, so there was barely any space between them. She was tall, so even though he outweighed her by almost a hundred pounds, he only had a couple of inches on her. She stared up at him, surprise and uncertainty in her eyes.

Then her gaze traveled down to his mouth and back up again, and there was something new in her expression, something that made him completely forget he'd ever been tired.

She was so different than anyone he'd ever known, and he'd had feelings for her practically since the day he'd started with SWAT. But he'd never made a move, even tried to keep his feelings for her hidden, because she was a teammate. He'd been wary of risking their friendship, wary of risking his place on the team where he'd just been accepted, wary of going in too soon and ruining his shot.

Then they'd become fast friends, and he absolutely knew there was no way he could ever have anything simple or temporary with this woman. And yeah, that was a little scary, too.

But right now, with her staring at him as if her feelings were just as strong, there was no way he could resist her.

She pressed her free hand against his chest, and it felt as if the world was moving in slow motion as she rose up on her tiptoes, and he leaned forward.

He brought his hand to the curve of her waist, marveling at how slender she was beneath all that lean muscle. His fingers slid up to the middle of her back, and he brought her even closer. His lips brushed lightly against hers, and he felt her sigh.

He could practically feel his whole world shifting beneath his feet as he made another pass over her lips with his, and then another, until her grip on his hand tightened, and she kissed him back, harder.

If he'd ever managed to keep his feelings for her hidden, the secret was definitely out now.

Then the door into the parking garage opened with a loud *bang* as it hit the wall, and Maggie jumped backward, fast.

The agent who'd come into the garage didn't even seem to notice them as he headed for his vehicle, but when Grant looked back at Maggie, she had taken another step back and was cursing under her breath.

Before he could say anything, she blurted, "That was a bad idea."

"I think it was one of the best ideas I've ever had."

He grinned at her, and she scowled back, her cheeks flushed. "Grant…" She shook her head. "We need to work together. Let's not make this messy."

"I'm okay with messy," he argued, moving toward her.

She held up a hand, and he stopped. "You're on my case. That changes things, whether you want it to or not. I need this guy caught before September."

Grant nodded, getting serious fast. "Okay." But come September 2, when they had the Fishhook Rapist in jail, he was going straight for messy, regardless of what it meant for his position on the SWAT team.

He'd been shocked when a spot had opened up as soon as he'd moved to DC—as though it was meant to be. The idea of leaving the team was like a punch to the gut. The guys—and Maggie—had become like family. A family he didn't want to lose. And the chance of getting onto one of the other SWAT teams without waiting *years* was minuscule at best. But the thought of not taking a chance with Maggie was worse.

"Do you have any solid leads on the case?"

He gaped at her. "Come on, Maggie. You know I can't tell you."

"Really?" Her hands went from being crossed over her chest to her hips. "Because you had no trouble breaking the rules a second ago."

"*You* kissed *me*," he argued.

"You sure about that?"

Was he? Jeez, he had no idea. "Look, Maggie, I promise you, we're doing everything we can—"

"I've been hearing that for a decade, Grant," she broke in. "And if this guy really is coming back for me, I want to be prepared."

Furious at the idea of the Fishhook Rapist getting anywhere near her again, he vowed, "We won't let that happen."

"Neither will I," she said, her battle face on. "So tell me something I can use."

He stared at her, at the stubborn set of her chin, and he knew. She was already investigating on her own.

He swore. "Maggie, this isn't your specialty. You should leave the case to Violent Crimes."

"Well, that's not happening. So help me or don't, but I'm still looking into it."

Worry gnawed at him. But he couldn't deny this was what he liked about her—her insistence on going full force at a problem.

As the only woman on their SWAT team, she could have gotten out of some of the particularly physically grueling jobs on an assignment, but she never did. Half the time, she volunteered for them. And they could always count on her to get it done, no question.

He took her hand, folding it into his before she could pull it back, and said, "Promise me if you come up with anything, you'll take me with you."

"Scott and Ella are helping me."

He should have realized. "Okay, fine. If you find anything, bring me or Scott. Agreed?"

She raised her eyebrows. "Take a guy with me? What about Ella?"

"She's a profiler, not an operator. Your brother is HRT. Promise me."

"Okay, I promise. I'm not stupid. I wouldn't chase after this guy on my own, not when he's after me specifically."

"Good." He looked down at their linked hands, then back into her gorgeous blue eyes. "We don't have anything solid yet, but if we find something, I'll share."

"Thank you." She eased her hand free. "I need to go."

As she walked away, Grant sighed heavily. When he'd been brought into this case, he'd promised he'd be able to uphold the confidentiality. Now, only a few days later, he was already promising Maggie that he'd break it.

The reality was, there was no way he could say no to her if she pressed him. And there was no way he could step away from the investigation, not when it was this important.

He had a bad feeling that before this case was over, his career was going to take a direct hit.

"WHERE WERE YOU?" Scott greeted her as she walked into her house.

Maggie jumped, even though she knew he'd be there, since his SUV was parked in her driveway. She'd given both Scott and Ella keys to her house, and they insisted on knowing her whereabouts every part of the day.

"I told you I was going to be late coming back from work." As soon as she'd gotten over the shock of discovering Grant was on the case, she'd decided to talk to him. That meant waiting around until he left, which hadn't been until nearly 7:00 p.m.

Then the whole drive home, she'd alternately berated and congratulated herself for kissing him. Yes, she'd wanted to do that for months. And she *had* been honest about how his being on the case changed things. Sure, if they'd somehow gotten around the problem of being teammates and started something serious, she would have told him about what had happened to her, eventually. But she would have given him the basics; she wouldn't have handed over pictures from her rape kit and every horrible detail from her interview with the cops a decade ago.

Even thinking about the fact that Grant knew such personal, painful things made a knot squeeze tighter in her chest.

Scott frowned at her. "You okay?"

"Yeah, I'm fine." She squinted at her brother, taking in the stress lines on his forehead that hadn't been there a few days ago, the dark circles under his eyes, then glanced at her watch. "You're early."

He turned away, saying, "Ella will be over in a bit. She was swinging home first to see Logan before he leaves for his shift."

Maggie's stomach growled, loudly, from being unable to eat much all day, and not wanting to go out for dinner and miss Grant leaving work.

"Ella's bringing dinner," Scott added.

Turning all the bolts behind her, Maggie hurried after him. "What aren't you telling me?"

"Nothing."

Maggie grabbed his arm, making him spin around. "Scott, what is it?"

He shuffled his feet, then sighed. "Nothing to do with your case. Don't worry about it."

He tried to pull his arm free, but she held on tighter. "I appreciate you and Ella trying to protect me, but I'd rather hear it straight. *What*?"

He smiled. "How is it that you always know when there's something I'm not saying, but I could tell Nikki I met an alien in the backyard and she'd believe me?"

Maggie rolled her eyes. Their younger sister had been coddled most of her life. A decade younger than Maggie, she'd already been the baby, but after Maggie's attack, the whole family had become even more protective of little Nikki. But for all her blind trust when it came to family, she wasn't a fool. Maggie and Scott had drilled safety techniques into her until she'd finally told them enough was enough, or she'd be paranoid about everyone she met. "She's not trained by the FBI. I am. And she's not *that* bad. So, spit it out."

"It has nothing to do with this case. I just bailed on some advanced defensive driving training I'd signed up for a long time ago. My supervisor isn't thrilled with me right now." Scott shrugged. "He'll get over it."

Maggie frowned, because this *was* about her. Six months ago, Ella had taken personal time and accepted a case on her own because she thought it was related to Maggie's abductor. Ella's supervisor had been surprisingly understanding, but Maggie knew it had cost Ella a lot of trust she'd worked hard to gain in the elite Behavioral Analysis Unit.

Now Scott was putting himself in a similar position. Again for her.

"Don't do that," Scott said. "I can read you just as well as you read me, sis. I make my own choices. And this really isn't a big deal."

She could tell he was lying, but she also knew it didn't matter what she said. There was no way her big brother—and one of her very best friends, to boot—was stepping one inch away from the case.

"Thanks" seemed so inadequate, but she didn't know what else to say.

He patted her arm as the growl of a convertible came closer. "I hear Ella. Let's eat and then figure out how to stop this guy for good."

"I'm on board with *that*," Maggie said, following him to the door to let in Ella, carrying bags of Chinese food.

An hour later, she, Ella and Scott sat cross-legged on the floor of her living room, surrounded by legal pads, laptops and discarded balls of paper.

"Okay, let's think about this," Ella suggested. "He picks a different state every year. These attacks are definitely specific, and he spends real time stalking the women first, which means he's not just flying out to a new state once a year. He's moving from year to year. So he's either got a job that allows him to travel without attracting notice, or he's got a lot of holes in his résumé."

"We've been through that," Scott said. "Salesman, pilot, trucker—"

"Trucker," Ella said, cutting him off. "What about a long-haul trucker? Maybe someone who's independent, who can pick his own routes. Because he definitely stalks his victims first. But a truck would give him a private location for the attacks and the branding. He could soundproof the back."

"I don't know," Maggie started, but Ella kept going.

"There's a reason the FBI put together that database

on Highway Serial Killers. The interstate travel means multiple jurisdictions that are harder to track, and the nature of the job means they're often around people who are high-risk victims."

"Sure," Scott said, "but aren't most of the victims who were in that database prostitutes? This guy goes for women who are at pretty low risk for being victims of a crime and at a high risk to himself."

Ella looked impressed. "You do listen when I babble about profiling, don't you?"

"Of course, kiddo," he said, using the nickname he'd had for her since childhood.

"I don't remember a truck," Maggie said quietly, and both of them got serious, looking over at her.

"Do you remember that part at all?" Scott asked.

Maggie had always told them both she couldn't remember much about her attack. And it was true. She just had fragments—nothing she'd ever thought would help in an investigation.

She recalled feeling dizzy as she walked out of the college party alone, as though she'd had way more to drink than just one beer. Then, later, being lifted off the ground after she'd tripped and fallen. A low voice, whispering in her ear right before the brand burned her neck. The vague sense of stumbling out of a vehicle before she dragged herself back to her dorm room.

She'd never remembered a face. Never remembered the assault itself. Nothing that would lead police to whoever had hurt her.

Even though she'd always felt some relief about that, she'd tried. She'd even let herself be hypnotized once, attempting to get back the details. But hospital staff and police experts had warned her that date-rape drugs like the one she'd consumed could eliminate huge chunks of time from her memory. They hadn't been surprised when she couldn't provide any details.

Still, for some reason she felt strongly about this part. "I only remember bits and pieces. I couldn't say for sure. But I just don't think I was in a truck."

"Well, a motel room is another possibility," Ella said. "Something off the beaten path a little, somewhere that charges by the hour and expects the sort of customer who'd prefer not to be remembered."

"Or he puts down roots, rents something for eight months then moves on to the next location and starts scouting," Maggie suggested.

"Which would mean he probably works odd jobs and has a résumé full of holes," Ella said. "And this perp is extremely intelligent. So in these odd jobs, he's either hiding that so he doesn't stand out, or he's noticed for it."

"I know the original profiler said he was antisocial," Maggie said. "So maybe he just keeps quiet."

"Yeah, maybe." Ella was frowning. "But we know he arrives sometime after September 1 in each new location, and he leaves before September 1 of the following year, probably at least a few months before, so he can pick out a new victim. So he's either choosing all short-term contract work, or he's suddenly going absent from these jobs and creating a trend."

"A trend we can track?" Scott asked skeptically.

"Probably not. But I'm not sure—"

"Or he's wealthy," Maggie cut in. "Wealthy enough that the money doesn't matter."

"Maybe," Ella said. "But the hook suggests something to do with water, so he could also have some sort of seasonal job in the fishing industry, something that ends before the fall."

"That makes a lot of sense," Scott agreed. "That hook has to mean something."

"Does it?" Maggie glanced between them, knowing her frustration was showing. "Or is he smart enough to do it to throw us totally off track?"

Her eyes were wet, and she blinked fast, hoping neither of them had noticed, but knowing they had. "What chance do we have of finding him? We don't even have the case files. Even the case agents—who worked nonstop all weekend—don't have any new leads."

"We're going to get him," Scott promised.

She nodded, hoping she looked as though she believed it. At work, she tackled every case assuming that if she just worked hard enough, she'd solve it. She tried to treat her own life the same way.

But year after year, the memories added up. Going through the same motions of gathering together and closing ranks with Ella and Scott. Watching the news even as they tried to stay away from it. Hoping that year would be different even when they knew it wouldn't.

And every year, it was exactly the same. Every year, she watched some new woman live out the same horrible thing she had, knowing that just like her, they'd only have partial memories. Knowing that just like her, they probably wouldn't be able to identify the Fishhook Rapist even if he walked right up to them.

In twenty-seven days, would the Fishhook Rapist walk right up to her? And if he did, would she know it before it was too late?

Chapter Five

Twenty days.

There were twenty days left until Maggie's attacker came back for her, and despite the best efforts of some of the most dedicated VCMO agents Grant knew, there were no new breaks in the case.

Despite his nonstop hours at work, poring over the evidence, he wasn't making a difference.

Grant slammed his fist against the wall of the van he was riding in, and the teammate seated next to him gave him a perplexed look.

"Grant!" Clive barked. "Get your head in the game."

"Sorry," he muttered, refocusing.

They were en route to a warehouse in a particularly bad area of DC, where case agents had determined a human trafficking ring was conducting business. Two of their supposed victims had already shown up in the morgue, burn marks on their bodies as apparent punishment before their throats were slit, and case agents expected more would surface unless they acted fast.

Maggie's squad had brought the warrants and the evidence, and requested SWAT for the potentially high-risk arrests. It was well after normal business hours, but surveillance indicated the personal vehicles of the three men listed on the arrest warrants were parked outside. The only three vehicles in the lot.

If SWAT was lucky, they'd be the only people inside the building tonight.

"They've got surveillance cameras everywhere, so we're hacking them and blocking the feed," Clive continued briefing them. "But if anyone's watching the cameras, they're going to know we're coming. So get your A-game ready, people."

Grant pushed Maggie's case to the back of his mind, but he couldn't help glancing at Maggie. She was squashed into the corner of the truck, and even in all her gear, she looked tiny next to the teammate they jokingly referred to as "Tank." Her dark hair curled around her chin underneath her helmet, and even with goggles dangling around her neck and buried underneath Kevlar and weaponry, she made his pulse pick up.

As the van bounced over potholes, she held her MP-5 and stared straight ahead, totally focused. And totally ignoring him, even though she probably felt his stare.

It had been that way for a week. It wasn't as if they weren't on speaking terms, but things were definitely strained between them, and had been since they'd kissed.

Still, he couldn't bring himself to regret it. Given the chance, he'd do it again.

He felt himself smile at the idea, and Maggie finally glanced his way as if she could sense the direction of his thoughts. But then she went back to staring straight ahead, which was typical for her right before a high-risk arrest.

Some of the guys worked off tension by joking around just before they went into a call—usually, he was one of them. Others on the team sat in silence. Maggie always seemed to be envisioning exactly how the raid was going to go.

It wouldn't surprise him if whatever she imagined was usually right—she tended to have a sixth sense on this kind of call. More than once, he'd watched her react to a threat before anyone else knew it was there, before there was any reason for her to know it existed. Some of the guys on the team called it "Maggie's Magic."

As they drove past the warehouse, giving them eyes on the target, he hoped for a little of that magic tonight. The quick look he had before the truck parked down the street was of a high chain-link fence topped with barbed wire, cameras mounted above the windowless doors, and three vehicles big enough to hold five people each parked close to the loading dock of the sprawling warehouse.

"Time to move," Clive said, nodding to the tech who was already typing away, preparing to black out the cameras.

Tank threw open the door, and six FBI SWAT agents jumped onto the street. As Grant fell into the front of the line, his adrenaline picked up. His regular position on VCMO was interesting and challenging, but SWAT—most of the time—was downright fun. Yeah, it was serious, but anyone who tried out for a SWAT team had to get a thrill from this kind of work.

As he took off down the street, he imagined anyone who happened to be in the decrepit building across the street looking outside and getting a shock. Normally, this area was pretty deserted after business hours, and for good reason. Even during the day, it wasn't the sort of place you'd want to wander into accidentally.

Just about every building on the block had been raided by FBI or local police or both at some point. But for every criminal they pushed out, another seemed to take his place. Gunshots weren't uncommon around here, but rarely did anyone call for help when they happened.

But six FBI agents decked out in combat gear, carrying heavy weaponry and a battering ram, running at full speed, had to make anyone with half a brain pray the targets were arrested quickly and without a fight.

Over his radio, the tech's tinny voice came through. "The target's cameras are down…now!"

Almost before he'd finished speaking, Clive was using bolt cutters on the lock keeping them on the wrong side of the fence. Then they passed through single-file and moved for the entry on the corner, the one with the least visibility for the occupants inside, and the best coverage for the agents, according to the blueprints they'd accessed.

As Clive fell to the back of the line, Maggie came up beside Grant, her MP-5 submachine gun up to cover him as he lifted the battering ram.

One solid hit, and the door flew inward, bouncing off the wall and almost closing on them again, until he smashed it back open with his foot. His night vision equipment lent an eerie green glow to the short, dark hallway, but it didn't illuminate any targets as Maggie stepped in first, moving past him quickly and off to his right.

Grant dropped the battering ram, raising his own primary weapon as he came up beside her. Then they were moving together, in a choreographed entry that felt like a thousand practice runs.

The rest of the team came in behind them, their combat boots clomping on the concrete floor as they moved quickly down the hall as a unit.

"Clear," Maggie's confident voice came through his headset as she opened a closet door on her side and checked it. Then they came up to the wide, open area that was the main part of the warehouse.

The agents began splitting off in twos, each into their own sectors. Much of the open warehouse space was filled floor to ceiling with boxes, providing plenty of places for targets to hide, and lots of places to clear. The area in his and Maggie's sector was open until it branched off down a separate hallway leading to offices.

Checking his peripherals because his teammates wouldn't be able to clear their sectors as quickly, Grant was surprised not to see anyone in the main area. Either the targets hadn't heard the entry—which they should have, with a battering ram—or they were hiding. Or everyone was in one of the two offices.

"Quiet," Maggie's voice whispered through his headset.

Too quiet was what he knew she meant.

He nodded once to acknowledge it, and then jutted his chin toward the door straight ahead. It was closed, but there was a light on inside. As they got closer, he could just make out a voice, and he strained to listen. It sounded like a scream, only turned down to almost nothing, as though it was coming from a TV.

"Possible target," he whispered as they both lifted their NVGs.

Maggie reached for the door handle with her left hand, keeping her weapon sighted with her right.

She turned the handle slowly, nodding as it moved on its own—meaning it wasn't locked. Then she shoved it open, giving him a view of one corner of the room, but no angle on the rest, as the muted scream became a high-pitched wail, full of pain. The soundproofed walls registered in his brain as a charred smell instantly filled his nostrils.

He watched Maggie's left hand go back to her weapon almost before the door opened, then watched her jaw go slack and her eyes go abnormally wide before her whole body froze.

Grant stepped sideways quickly, the rest of the room coming into view. The filthy, half-dressed woman on the floor, a man's knee pressed into her back as he held a lighter to her. Another man standing beside him, looking bored. And a third behind them, surprise on his face as he yanked up a pistol.

Grant heard himself screaming at the target to put it down, even as he lurched sideways, shoving Maggie out of the doorway and trying to sight his weapon at the same time.

He pulled the trigger, then something smashed into his chest, and he flew through the air as a pair of gunshots filled his ears. He slammed into the ground with enough force that it would have knocked the air out of his lungs, if he could actually breathe. His head hit the ground, and his vision dimmed as he gasped for oxygen and groped with his left hand for the source of the pain exploding in his chest.

From what seemed like a long distance away, he heard Maggie's voice screaming his name, and two more gunshots in rapid succession. Then a dark figure filled his vision, and he tried to blink it into focus, tried to lift the weapon he was pretty sure was still clutched in his right hand, as his fingers finally grazed over his chest and dipped into the bullet hole.

"Grant!"

Panic filled Maggie's chest as she slung her MP-5 over her back, dropped to her knees and reached for the hand Grant had clasped over his chest. His eyes were rolled back in his head, but he kept blinking as though he was trying to focus, and gasping for breath.

Please let him be okay, a voice chanted in her head, as she tried to remember all the training that had become second nature over the past four years in SWAT. Never in those four years had she watched a teammate take a bullet.

"Where are you hit?" she yelled, even though she knew he couldn't answer her.

She didn't wait for him to try. Instead, she pushed his hand aside, relief flooding through her as she saw the bullet lodged near the top of his Kevlar vest. But that didn't mean it hadn't caused damage.

Forcing her hand underneath his vest, she searched for any sign the bullet had gone through. But there was no blood.

Still, it was possible he had a collapsed lung, or broken ribs, or...

"I'm okay." Grant interrupted her fears as he finally seemed to catch his breath and started to push himself up.

"Stay there," Maggie said, but he ignored her, getting to a sitting position and looking around, already back on task as he checked for new threats.

"Status? Maggie, status?"

Suddenly realizing the question was coming from both Grant beside her and Clive over her headset, Maggie replied, "Grant was hit in the vest." Her heart still raced as she tried to get it together, tried not to think about what could have happened, tried not to think about *why*.

She'd never let anything distract her from a mission before. Never let her history prevent her from doing her job. Until today.

There'd be plenty of time to berate herself later. Right now she needed to get her mind back on the mission.

"Three targets down. One victim needs an ambulance."

"And Grant?" Clive pressed.

"I'm okay," Grant told them both.

Maggie glanced at him where he sat on the floor, still wincing as he braced a hand against his chest. "Grant, I'm sor—"

"Not now," he said, getting to his feet with a lot more effort than it should have taken.

"Are you sure you don't need—"

"It'll be a nasty bruise. Nothing's broken. Let's check the room." He slung his own MP-5 over his back, grunting at the movement, and grabbed the Glock strapped to his thigh then moved toward the room.

Reluctantly, she unholstered her own Glock, better for close quarters than the MP-5, and followed, looking into the office.

Inside, the three men who were listed on their warrants were down for good, one from Grant's bullet and two from hers. The three traffickers had only gotten two shots off, the one that had hit Grant and another that had gone wide, passing over her right shoulder.

There was nowhere in the office to hide. The only other person in the room was the woman who'd picked herself up off the floor and was cowering in the corner, rocking back and forth. Surely one of the trafficking victims.

The smell hit Maggie as soon as she entered. Not the blood. The burning.

She fought back the urge to gag, fought the memory that tried to incapacitate her a second time. The same memory that had surged forward the instant she'd opened the door. A memory she hadn't even realized she possessed.

A memory that had very nearly gotten Grant killed.

She glanced at him, checking the pulses on the three men on the floor, even though they were clearly gone. It chilled her how close he'd come to dying outside this room.

He looked back at her, concern and a hint of pain in his deep brown eyes, and she couldn't hold his gaze.

"Our sector's clear," Grant said into his mic, and within the next few minutes, the rest of the team announced the same.

"We've got ERT, an ambulance and the coroner on the way," Clive told them. "They're less than a minute out. We're coming to you now."

Before the team made it into the room, Grant had checked the woman over for any serious injuries—and weapons, because you could never assume—and Maggie had cuffed the three perps with the zip ties looped on her belt. Dead or not, it was procedure.

The whole time, she tried not to breathe too deeply.

"You okay?" Clive asked Grant as he joined them in the office, the rest of the team behind him, looking shaken. This was the first time anyone on the team had been shot since before Maggie had joined four years ago.

"I'm good," Grant replied easily, already beginning to move around as if he hadn't taken a bullet to the chest.

Vest or not, at this range, that had to *hurt*. A few inches higher, and it could have been much, much worse.

Was he playing it down because that was a SWAT agent's way? Or because of her?

"What happened?" Clive asked.

Grant opened his mouth, but Maggie cut him off, not wanting to know what he was going to say. Not wanting him to tell Clive she'd frozen at a critical moment, but not wanting him to lie for her, either.

"It was my fault," she said, watching her teammates'

eyes widen behind Clive as they looked back and forth between her and Grant and the dead men on the floor.

Grant frowned, his attention darting to the woman in the corner of the room, and Maggie realized he'd put it all together.

Of course he had. He'd read all the details from her case file. He knew exactly what had happened to her a decade ago, every terrible detail. Including the brand on the back of her neck.

It had smelled the same today as it had ten years ago, when she'd heard a voice whispering in her ear, telling her something would hurt. As she'd struggled toward consciousness to find her head pressed against a cold, hard surface. A hand against the back of her head. A disorienting, numb feeling over her entire body, and complete confusion as a room slowly came into focus around her. A room she didn't recognize. And then a sudden, fierce pain at the back of her neck, and the smell of her own skin burning.

She tried to force back the memory, then looked up at Clive and blurted out words she never thought she'd say. "I need to leave the SWAT team."

Chapter Six

"I'm so sorry."

Maggie blurted the words as soon as Grant opened his door. The door she'd finally gotten the courage to knock on after standing on his front stoop for ten minutes in the glow of the porch light.

She'd never been to his house before, but she'd told Ella and Scott not to come over tonight, because she was going out with her SWAT friends. There'd be plenty of time to break the news to them later about her sudden career change.

Instead, she'd looked up Grant's address and made the surprisingly short drive to his house.

Grant opened the door wide and stepped aside. His voice was somber when he said, "Come in, Maggie." He sounded as if he'd expected her, as though maybe he'd been waiting up for her.

Nerves, guilt and regret mingled as she stepped inside, glancing around. His tidy little row house looked similar to hers on the outside, but inside it was very different. Hardwood floors instead of carpet, beige walls instead of the muted blues and greens and yellows she'd chosen. More sparsely decorated, but somehow it still felt cozy.

She followed him into the living room, and her eyes

were immediately drawn to a row of pictures over his fireplace. She couldn't stop herself from stepping closer.

One was clearly him in high school, because he was wearing a letter jacket. He'd been muscular even as a teenager, and he had his arms around two smaller boys, a tired-looking black woman behind them. The younger boys took after their mother where Grant, who seemed to have some strong Mediterranean heritage, probably resembled his father. Still, there was something so similar in their expressions, marking them as siblings. The pictures on either side were of those boys grown up, married, little kids on their knees.

Grant stood next to her, his shoulder brushing hers. "My younger brothers." He pointed to the pictures on the outsides of the little boys, pride in his voice. "And this is them now, with my nephews."

She looked back at the young boys, his brothers' kids, who looked like miniature versions of Grant, and an ache settled somewhere inside that she didn't want to acknowledge. She'd never really let herself think about kids, because she'd never been able to get anywhere near the point of wanting to have them with someone.

"And your mom?" Maggie asked, looking at the center picture again, the one where Grant's expression said he'd grown up fast. Too fast. Even as a teenager, the protective instinct nearly screamed from him. The same way it did now, on SWAT.

"Yeah. Not the greatest picture of her, but it was one of the first family photos we have from after my dad took off. I need to get something more recent up there before she comes to visit and gets mad at me for choosing that picture to put up."

He grinned at her, and she couldn't help it. There was something about the way he smiled, the way it made his eyes brighten, the way he seemed to grin with his whole face, every time, that always made her smile back.

But it faded fast. "Grant, I owe you—"

"Nothing." He cut her off, actually sounding as if he meant it. "You owe me nothing."

"I owe you a lot more than just an apology. I wish I could go back to the day Clive asked me if I wanted to take time off from SWAT and—"

"Stop it," Grant said, and it wasn't his words, but the fact that he actually put his finger over her lips that made her quiet.

The touch sent a tingling feeling outward over her face, and his expression changed, too. The serious veneer was gone, replaced with a mixture of emotions she couldn't begin to unravel. But worry and desire were definitely part of the mix.

His gaze dropped to her lips, and instead of moving his finger, he traced it slowly over her mouth.

Every pore on her body seemed to suddenly come alive as the tingling swept outward, down to her toes. She stepped back fast. "What are you doing? I got you *shot* today!"

He walked over to the oversize leather couch on the far wall and sat down. "You're human. Everyone makes mistakes, Maggie."

She stared down at him incredulously. "You can't be serious!"

"I've messed up clearing a room before."

"Did you get someone else shot?" she demanded.

"No. I got lucky." He leaned forward, taking his arms off the back of the couch where he'd rested them as though he was settling in for a long argument. "Ask any guy on the team, and I bet you'll hear the same thing."

She frowned. Maybe that was true, maybe not, but it

was irrelevant. Her actions had gotten a teammate shot. And it didn't matter that he was okay. It didn't matter that it had happened because of a memory she couldn't have predicted would rear its ugly head at exactly the wrong time. What mattered was that it had happened.

"If I hadn't quit tonight, I would have been off the team, anyway."

"You would have been talking to OPR," Grant countered. The Bureau's Office of Professional Responsibility, who would investigate tonight's incident, got involved whenever a firearm was used. "Just like you're doing now. But you'll come through this, and you need to *fight* for your spot on the team, Maggie. You belong there, and we all know it. Besides, I'm fine. No harm, no foul."

She gaped at him. "How can you be this calm about getting shot?"

"It hurt less than being stabbed."

A burst of laughter escaped. "You should be pissed at me right now. What's wrong with you? You should hate me!"

"It wasn't you who shot me," Grant said, still so calmly it was starting to piss *her* off.

"No, it was me who *got you* shot!"

"And I'm glad it was me who was hit." He leaned toward her and held out his hand. "Come here."

"What?" She shook her head, not moving. "Why?"

He rolled his eyes, stood up and peeled his T-shirt off, tossing it aside. "Look." He put his hand up at the top of his chest, where a huge purple bruise spread outward from a dark center to a lighter bluish color snaking toward his neck.

She'd seen him without his shirt on before, but always in training, surrounded by a group of other FBI agents, including herself, all keeping in shape for missions. Times when she'd purposely avoided looking. Nothing like the sudden intimacy here, alone with him in his home.

Her mouth suddenly felt dry. She couldn't stop her eyes from wandering over football-player shoulders, down biceps that bulged with muscle without even being flexed, to what should have been a six-pack but looked more like a twelve-pack.

Her fingers pulsed with the need to reach out and stroke the bruise, or the shiny, jagged scar that ran along his side—a present from the Manhattan Strangler. From there, she could trace her fingers up to the ridges of muscle on his abdomen. She could glide her hands over him until he truly forgave her for what had happened in that warehouse tonight.

"Maggie." He sounded amused, but when she forced herself to look up, heat lit his eyes.

"Sorry," she whispered.

He strode toward her, and common sense told her to flee, but he was standing in front of her before she could move, so close she could feel the heat from his body.

She bit her lip as she felt his hand close around hers, lifting it up. He placed it over his bruise, and just as her fingers started to open, he moved her hand back toward her.

In an instant, she realized why he'd told her he was glad it had been him who'd gotten shot. It had happened because she'd frozen, but if he hadn't shoved her out of the way, she'd have been the one with a bullet hole.

Her fingers drifted over the base of her neck, neatly lined up with the bruise on the top of Grant's chest. No vest would have saved her.

The knowledge left her suddenly cold. The cold intensified as Grant turned and walked away, grabbing his T-shirt off the couch and slipping it over his head.

When he settled back on his couch and gestured for her to join him, this time her feet moved slowly until she was sitting next to him. "That doesn't make me feel any better."

"Well, you're going to have to deal with it. And you have enough to focus on right now, so stop worrying. I'm fine. You're fine. And once you go through all the OPR stuff, we want you back. *I* want you back."

Maggie shook her head, but he insisted, "Don't decide now. But just so you know, everyone on the team agrees."

She was touched by their loyalty, and surprised. Because on SWAT, decisions about teammates had nothing to do with friendship, and everything to do with ability. But it didn't matter how they felt. She had to do what was right for the team, whether they saw it or not.

"I'm a liability." It killed her to admit it, but right now, it was true. And she didn't remember much at all from her attack, so how could she predict if that would happen again, some other memory getting triggered at the wrong time?

Grant took her hand in his. "Once this case is closed and you've got your focus back, you'll change your mind."

"You're too nice for your own good. You know that, right? You know it's not normal to ask the person who just got you shot to come back and cover you?"

"I'll let you cover me anytime you want."

More laughter snuck out at the completely out-of-character remark, and she shifted to face him on the couch. "Are you actually hitting on me right now? Because your pickup lines could use some work."

"Really?" He turned slightly, moving a little closer and

stroking his fingers over the palm of her hand, igniting her nerve endings with the simple touch. "The way you were drooling before, I thought it'd be okay."

"I was *not* drooling," she said, even as she felt heat in her cheeks. But she found herself smiling back at him.

How did he always do that to her? Even on a day like today, with everything going on, with the shooting and the memories and the guilt she was feeling? How could he still make her feel this ridiculous, giddy happiness?

"Maybe you're right," she whispered, suddenly desperate to feel his lips on hers the way they had been in the parking lot of the WFO a week ago.

She leaned toward him, fast, before she could change her mind. Moving in close, she pressed her mouth to his.

And just like the last time they'd kissed, all rational thought fled her mind, and she could only focus on Grant. The bunching muscles underneath her hand, the tiny rasp of stubble from his chin, the ridiculous softness of his lips.

She moved even closer, until she was plastered against him, and could slide both her arms around his neck. Until she could open her mouth, inviting his tongue inside.

He didn't hesitate, and the first brush of his tongue against hers left her desperate for more. She tried to lean even closer, and felt his hands slip underneath her thighs and lift her up onto his lap as though she weighed nothing.

She tried to wriggle closer still, and felt the rumble of his laughter as his hands locked on her hips and held her still. She thought she heard him mutter something about his self-control—or maybe it was hers—and then he was kissing her again, flooding her entire body with need.

She ran her hands down over his arms then underneath his T-shirt, wanting to feel his bare skin again, this time wanting to caress her fingers over all the muscles she'd seen earlier.

He sucked in a breath as her fingers followed the lines of muscle in his abdomen up to his chest, stopping just short of his bruise, and she flattened her hand there, loving the feel of his heart thumping madly underneath her fingers. She wanted more.

Wrenching her mouth from his, she panted, "Bedroom," then leaned back in, hoping he'd just stand up and take her there.

Instead, his hands moved up to her waist, skirting around the gun at her hip, and he didn't let her close the distance to his lips again. "Maggie," he whispered, his voice even deeper than usual. "Maybe this isn't a good idea."

Surprise and embarrassment flooded. What was she thinking? She'd gotten him shot, then tried to sleep with him in the same night?

She tried to move off his lap, but his hands were still tight on her waist, holding her in place.

Of course this wasn't a good idea. Now that Grant knew everything he knew about her past, it was only a matter of time before it colored the way he looked at her. And she wasn't the type to sleep with someone without being in a relationship. Not anymore. Not in a long, long time.

"I'm sorry," she muttered, dropping her hands off his shoulders. "Let's forget this ever happened."

GRANT CURSED AS Maggie flushed deep red, trying to get off him.

"I just meant the timing, Maggie. Not that I'm not interested." Which should have been pretty obvious.

She still looked mortified—and as if she didn't quite

believe him—so he slid one hand up her back until he could pull her toward him and capture her mouth with his again.

He'd intended to kiss her fast, just once more, then convince her that they should wait until after her case was solved. Because a relationship between them was complicated enough already, with work, and especially now, with the inevitable OPR investigation into today's SWAT call. But add in her flashback and everything happening with her case, and he didn't want to screw things up for later by jumping in at the worst possible time.

But as soon as his lips found hers, longing rocked through him, a reminder of everything he'd been wanting for the past nine months. Everything he'd been looking for since before he even met her. *Maggie.*

He must have said her name out loud, probably sounding as desperate as he felt, because she mumbled something in return, then brought her mouth to his again. A second later, she shifted, until he could feel her whole body against his.

And he knew right then that it would take way more willpower than he possessed to say no to her again. But he pulled away from her long enough to whisper, "How about you take this off?"

She blinked back at him, and he patted her holster so she'd know what he was talking about.

She looked a little disappointed, so he added, "I'd prefer to take the rest off myself."

She smiled, but he didn't miss the brief indecision in her expression before she unstrapped her holster.

As she leaned over to drop her weapon on his side table, he forced himself to say, "Maggie, we can—"

"Shut up, Grant," she replied, wrestling his shirt off and tossing it on the floor. Then she sat there staring at him, eyebrows raised, as if she was waiting for him to make good on his promise.

Remembering how she'd responded before when he'd stroked his fingers over her palm, he reached for her hand and pressed it to his lips, tracing a circle on her palm with his mouth and his tongue until she relaxed toward him. Then he stroked his other hand up underneath the back of her T-shirt, marveling that someone who could handle an MP-5 the way she did had such silky, soft skin.

She squirmed on his lap and took her hand from his lips, hooking it onto his shoulder as she leaned into him again.

Tilting his head, he kissed her harder, drawing her T-shirt up. Then he stopped kissing her long enough to slip it over her head. He got a brief glimpse of a blue satin bra the same shade as her eyes, and then her bare skin was against his, and he groaned.

She smiled back at him, a pleased smile that told him she knew exactly what she was doing to him right now, and then she dipped her head, and he felt her lips on his earlobe. As her tongue slid across his neck, he felt his self-control slipping further and further out of reach.

Frantic with the need to kiss her again, he slid his hand up her back, so he could glide his fingers through her hair and tilt her head back to his. Just before his fingers reached the back of her neck, he realized what he was doing. A jolt hit him at his mistake, and he froze.

He tried to recover and skip over her neck to just palm the back of her head, but it was too late.

Hurt showed in her eyes as she stood up. She bumped his coffee table hard enough that it was probably going to leave a bruise, but she didn't seem to notice as she grabbed her T-shirt off the floor and pulled it over her head.

"I'm sorry." He got to his feet, too, dread pooling in his stomach.

"And you said knowing about my past didn't change anything."

He shook his head, genuinely bewildered. "It doesn't."

"Right." She turned away from him, picking up her holster and strapping it back on.

"Maggie." He put his hand on her arm, and felt her muscles tense. "It doesn't change how I *feel* about you. I just didn't think you'd want me touching you there. That's all."

She looked up at him, hurt and frustration written on her face, but he could see the truth of his words register there, too.

She wore her hair short enough that it wouldn't be a hassle in SWAT, but long enough to cover the entire back of her neck. It was a logical assumption she wouldn't want any man touching the brand there.

She stepped backward, making him drop her arm. "If it really didn't matter, you wouldn't be thinking about that at all. You'd be focused on me. On us. On right now."

"That's not fair," he countered. "After what happened today—"

She cut him off, swearing. She was practically yelling, but she sounded more frustrated than angry when she said, "I'm so sick of this. Every year. Every single year, I'm just sitting around waiting to see who's next." She dropped onto his couch, something defeated in the hunch of her shoulders he'd never seen before. "And this year, it's me again."

He sat next to her, wrapping an arm around her shoulder even as she tensed up at his touch. "It's *not* going to be you again. This is all going to be over soon."

"It'll never be over." She turned her head, looking

away from him, then admitted, her voice cracking, "I *don't* like anyone touching my neck."

He could feel her arms trembling as she said, so quietly he had to lean in to hear, "I had to go back six times before I could manage to get the tattoo over it."

"But you did it."

"Yeah, well, I wasn't going to let him win. No way was I leaving that mark on my body."

She turned away from him even more, lifting his arm off her shoulder. But when he'd expected her to stand up and leave, she tilted her head down and lifted her hair.

He'd seen the pictures from the case file, when the brand was new. Red and angry, an ugly raised hook on her delicate neck.

Now the damaged skin underneath was still evident if you looked closely enough, but she'd had a tattoo—some Chinese letters—put directly on top of it. Something that must have been incredibly difficult to do, but that was Maggie. She never backed down from any challenge.

"What does it mean?" he asked, as she dropped her hair back down to cover the deep black symbol inked on her neck.

"Strength," she answered, getting to her feet.

"Good choice," he said as she turned to face him. It was probably the most appropriate thing she could have chosen. She was one of the strongest people he knew.

She nodded, and from the raw look in her eyes, he suspected she very rarely showed it to anyone.

"Can you tell me what you remembered today?" he asked. He'd planned to do it tomorrow, but he suddenly didn't want to make her talk about it at the office.

"I figured we'd get to that eventually," she said then sat back down at the far corner of the couch, away from him. She glanced at him briefly, then away. "Can you put a shirt on?"

"Okay." He picked up his T-shirt from the floor and put it back on, then settled in the center of the couch, giving her the distance she obviously wanted.

"It was the smell." She was looking straight ahead, not at him, but he could tell she was wearing her SWAT-ready expression.

"I figured," he said softly. Scent was one of the most powerful triggers for memory.

"I thought I'd remembered everything I'd ever get back about that day—which wasn't much," she said, then shook her head, and her voice was stronger, more detached when she continued. "But today I remembered a room. I'd never been there before. It was...fancy. My head was on a table, a really cold table." She frowned, looking pensive, and then finally nodded, adding, "I think it was marble."

A marble table? Definitely not a pay-by-the-hour type motel or in a vehicle. Which lent credence to his theory that the person who'd done this had actually lived in DC when he'd attacked Maggie, and that he hadn't just been passing through searching for a victim.

"The room was blurry. From the drugs."

Grant tried to ignore the fury that rose up as Maggie talked, at the idea of anyone drugging her, hurting her. But it rose up like bile in his throat.

"I'm not sure I'd recognize it if I saw it today. But there were pictures on the wall, big ones, nice frames. And carpet under my knees. Thick carpet. I think it was a large room." She shuddered when she added, "When I screamed, it echoed."

"Do you remember anything about him?" Grant asked, trying to keep the anger out of his voice.

But she must have heard it, because she turned and looked at him. He thought she was going to say something—not about the case, but about his reaction—but after a long pause, she just shook her head.

"He was behind me. With the—with whatever he used on my neck. I think I passed out again after that." She paused. "I still don't remember him."

"Well, this could help," he told her. "These are new details. And I think…"

"What?" she demanded when he cut himself off before he blurted out his case theories.

"It could help."

"I told you all that, and that's all you're giving me?"

"You know I'm not supposed to—"

"What?" she interrupted. "Make out with a teammate?"

Even though he knew she was pissed, he couldn't help smiling at that. "Well, yeah, that, too."

"Come on. You already know I'm investigating. We have twenty days." She looked at her watch "Make that nineteen. I may not be VCMO, but I spend my days investigating some nasty stuff, too. Don't waste resources. Tell me what you're thinking."

Despite the voice screaming in his head that this was a really bad idea, screaming that she was using his feelings for her to get case information she'd never have access to otherwise, he told her. "I think he started in DC. I think you were the first one he marked, but not his first victim."

She frowned back at him. "Yeah, Ella thinks that, too, about him having a history of rape. Not necessarily about DC."

"Well, I think whoever he started with was someone in his life, and that her attack is why the date is significant."

She stared back at him, nodding slowly. "Maybe."

"If I'm right—"

"There could be a way to track him," she finished.

Chapter Seven

Maggie was sitting up in bed, her hand already gripping her gun, before she'd even identified what had woken her. Her heart thudding, she glanced at her alarm clock—6:00 a.m.

Below her, from outside, a car door slammed. Her bedroom faced the street, but there wasn't a lot of traffic quite this early, not where she lived.

Getting out of bed, she moved beside the window, lifting the slats on the blinds to peer outside. She saw Grant walking up her drive at the same moment she heard movement from inside her house, on the first floor.

Where her overprotective brother had spent the night on her couch. He'd been there, half-asleep, when she'd gotten home from Grant's house last night. For once, she'd managed to avoid his questions and go straight to bed.

She doubted Grant had already been to work, or had a break in the case, which meant he was probably stopping by on his way to the WFO. And that meant he either wanted to talk about her quitting SWAT or what had happened between them last night.

She felt momentarily frozen watching him stride up her driveway, until she heard another thud from downstairs. Probably Scott preparing to confront any approaching threats.

Cursing, she let the blinds drop and ran down the stairs. "Scott, it's just—"

Before she'd finished speaking, her brother had swung open the front door and tucked his gun into the waistband of his pants. "Grant."

"Scott, hi." Grant held out a hand for her brother, looking surprised.

"Scott and Ella alternate staying with me until this whole thing is over," Maggie reminded Grant, her words coming out too fast, and she felt herself flush as his gaze locked on hers. After last night, even his eyes on her gave her goose bumps.

Scott gave her a questioning look as he shook Grant's hand, and she remembered she hadn't told him that Grant was working the case.

"Come on in," Scott said, stepping back and rubbing his eyes. "You guys have a call or something?"

Grant frowned as he walked inside. "No. Didn't Maggie tell—"

"Is there something new with the case?" she asked, willing him not to tell her brother she'd left SWAT.

"No. I'm sorry. I just, uh—"

So he'd come by to clear the air about last night. After she'd told him the details of her flashback, things had suddenly felt awkward in a way they never, ever had with Grant. Not until he'd started investigating her case. She'd had a desperate need to get out of there, so she had, quickly, with barely a goodbye.

She'd known seeing him in the office today was going to be uncomfortable. She should have figured Grant would do this.

"Sorry I ran out on you last night," she said, hoping her

brother would assume the "you" she was talking about was plural—the whole team. "It was a long day."

"Sure, that's okay," Grant said slowly.

Maggie tried to appear nonchalant when Scott looked at her.

Grant was terrible at deception. He'd be an awful undercover agent.

It was a good thing he'd gone into VCMO and SWAT, where he could use his size and pissed-off expression to terrify the criminals, and his easygoing, contagious smile to reassure the victims, or charm his way into a tight-knit SWAT team. Or into her affections.

"I'm going to grab a coffee," Scott said in an obvious move to give them privacy. "Nice to see you, Grant." As he walked past Maggie, he raised his eyebrows, and she knew she'd be getting grilled as soon as Grant left.

"You, too," Grant called after him, then quieter, to her, "You haven't told him?"

"No," she whispered back. "But now I'll have to, because it's pretty obvious something's up." She shook her head at him, moving closer so her brother wouldn't overhear. "You're a terrible liar."

"He caught me off guard."

"I told you he was staying with me." Suddenly conscious of the fact that she was wearing pajama pants and a snug tank top without anything underneath, she crossed her arms over her chest. Instead of asking him why he was there, she said, "Can we talk later?"

"Yeah, I wasn't thinking about your brother being here. I totally forgot. I just wanted to see you, to—"

"To clear the air about last night," she said, staring at the collar of his T-shirt, where a hint of his bruise was visible. "I get it. But things are fine between us, okay?"

"No, I came by to apologize."

Surprised, she looked up at him, and he stepped closer still, close enough that she could smell his citrusy aftershave. She resisted the urge to breathe deeply, resisted the urge to lean into him the way she had last night. She'd gotten him shot, and now *he* wanted to apologize? "About what?"

"My timing."

She could feel herself gaping at him as he continued, "I waited nine months to do that. I could have waited another three weeks, until this case was over. I'm sorry."

"You waited nine months," she said slowly, "to—"

"To kiss you."

The flush she'd felt the second he walked through her door doubled. "We *met* nine months ago."

He grinned at her. "Yeah, I know. I walked into that first SWAT meeting, and you introduced yourself, and that was it."

"Introduced myself? I flipped you."

It was standard ops to prank the new guy. And since she'd joined the team, one of her teammates' favorite ways to initiate the newbies was for her to walk up, hold out a limp hand for them to shake, then promptly flip them to the ground.

In the three years before Grant joined that she'd been part of the team, she'd gone along with it because she found it was a good way to stop any preferential treatment before it could start. Drop a guy on his very first day on SWAT, and he wasn't likely to go easy on her just because she was a woman.

The four guys she'd flipped before Grant had been pissed off and embarrassed, but they'd gotten over it and become her friends. Grant had actually pulled her down with him. When they'd landed, with her braced on top of him, he'd looked stunned for a second, then offered her a hand as he'd gotten to his feet, laughing.

Oddly enough, that was the moment she'd fallen for him.

"Yeah, well, I like a woman who knows how to be in control. Besides," he said, leaning close to whisper, just as she heard her brother walk back into the room behind her, "I'm okay with you being on top."

She stammered something unintelligible as he backed up, nodded at her brother and walked out the door.

"What was that about?" Scott asked.

"Nothing," Maggie answered, but her voice came out way too high.

"Uh-huh," Scott said, "nice try. What's going on?"

Hoping she wasn't still blushing furiously, Maggie turned around. "Work stuff."

Scott snorted. "Come on. What's happening? And while you're telling me what's up with Grant, you want to fill me in on what you told Nikki?"

"Nikki? What are you talking about?"

"She called. Asked me about coming to visit in a few weeks. She wanted to be here September 1. I thought maybe you'd said something—"

"No way," Maggie said. "I didn't tell her about the letters. Did you?"

"No. And I told her to stay home, obviously. I said she should focus on her new job and getting settled in her new place. But I was surprised she volunteered."

"She's growing up." It *was* surprising, though, not because Nikki was insensitive, but because they'd always tried to keep her far away from their horrible September 1 ritual. And Maggie wanted to keep it that way.

"Okay, well, she'll probably call you. I told her not to come, but I don't think she was ready to give up."

"I'll handle her," Maggie said.

"Okay, and what about Grant? I don't know the guy all that well, but he was acting unusually cagey. And he knows about the Fishhook case? What didn't he want to say in front of me? If there's something about the case you're keeping from me—"

"It's not that. I mean, yes, I remembered something new about what happened to me, but it doesn't help with the case."

"You remembered more?" Scott sounded surprised. "Are you sure it won't help us? Because whatever it is, I don't want to be in the dark on this, Maggie. I can't help if I don't know everything."

"He wasn't here about the case. Although he's been assigned to it."

Scott's eyes narrowed with suspicion. "Is there something going on between you two?"

"I'm off SWAT," she blurted, not needing an overprotective brother to mess up her already rocky love life. And she definitely wasn't ready to talk about whatever was happening with Grant.

"What?" Scott set his coffee down, his face going pale. "What happened yesterday? Are you okay?"

"I made a mistake. It was bad, and I'm going to have to answer for it with OPR." Before he could dig for details, she added, "I quit the team."

She tried not to think about what that meant. Sure, she was dedicated to her regular work on the civil rights squad, but she *loved* SWAT. She had from the moment she'd been accepted onto the team.

"What? Maggie, what happened? I'm sure you can—"

"I'll give you the awful details later, okay?" She dreaded the idea of telling him about those ten crucial seconds when she'd frozen. HRT training was even more intensive than SWAT, and her brother had never made the kind of error she'd made today. On top of his ever-present worry about her, she didn't want to see disappointment on his face.

She ducked her head as he stared at her as if he could read the answer on her face if he looked long enough. Suddenly wishing Ella were here instead of her brother, Maggie sighed. At least with Ella, if she said she needed a little space, she'd get it. With Scott, *not* telling him something just made him even more persistent.

But for once, he backed off. She could tell he had a hard time getting the words out as he said, "Okay. Just tell me if you need anything. Ella, too." He squeezed her arm. "We're here for you. We always will be."

Tears stung the backs of her eyes as she nodded. They'd stuck by her for a decade, changing the whole course of their lives and joining the Bureau because of her. Every September 1, they dropped everything to be by her side. Now they were secretly investigating the Fishhook Rapist case with her because she couldn't leave it to the case agents.

Meanwhile, she was making errors at work she'd never, ever allowed herself to make before. Errors that would threaten not only her place on SWAT, but if she wasn't careful, her place in the Bureau, too.

And if she let Scott and Ella, they'd go down with her, like a sinking ship.

"What do you want?"

The woman peering suspiciously at him looked nothing like the picture Grant had in a police file from thirteen years ago.

She'd only opened her door an inch or two, so he held his badge a little closer to her, and repeated, "I'm with the

FBI. I wanted to ask you a few questions about a crime you reported a long time ago that might be connected to a current investigation."

She shook her head, limp peroxide-blond hair swinging. "I never reported any crime."

"It was a sexual assault report."

"Oh." Her shoulders slumped, and she glanced quickly behind her, then opened the door wide. Instead of inviting him in, she came outside, shutting the door behind her. Folding her arms, she said, "I don't want my kids to hear this." Then she squinted at him and asked, "What do you want to know about that? It was a really long time ago." Her shoulders lifted. "They never figured out who did it."

"Is there anyone *you* suspected?" Grant asked hopefully.

This was his third stop this morning. It would have been more, but only a handful of the possible matching cases had victims still in the area.

It was actually a little scary how many rape cases in the five years prior to Maggie's assault happened on or around September 1 in the DC area. He'd been able to narrow it down to the Fishhook Rapist's victim type— women in their late teens to early twenties, with long, dark hair. Which had given him three possibilities.

So far, no one he'd talked to had been able to give him anything new. Shana Mills, the woman standing in front of him now, was his most likely option, but even she was just a slim possibility. Given how under-reported rape was, chances were that even if his theory was right, and the Fishhook Rapist had assaulted women before he'd gotten his media name, they probably wouldn't have a police report for it.

"I don't have any ideas," Shana replied. "Not any more than I did back then. I was drugged. To be honest, I wasn't even totally certain what had happened until the doctors confirmed it."

"So you don't remember anyone?"

"No."

He glanced at the notes he'd jotted from the police file. Three years before Maggie's assault, Shana Mills had been drugged and raped. He'd almost missed it when he'd been digging through the DCPD's files, because she hadn't gone to the hospital until September 2, and the official police report hadn't been filed until later.

The investigation had been almost nonexistent, because the police had little to go on. Shana didn't remember her assailant; he'd worn a condom, and Shana had woken up in the basement of a frat house the morning after a big party. Lots of possible suspects, lots of potential witnesses, but no one had seen a thing, and the evidence hadn't been there.

"What can you tell me about Jeffrey Hoffmeier and Kevin Sanders?" Those were the only names listed in the police report who were possible suspects in his current case, since they were the only ones with a personal connection to Shana. That was assuming Grant's attempt at a profile of the Fishhook Rapist was right. It wasn't his specialty, but he'd put together a solid profile before, with the Manhattan Strangler, so he had to trust his gut.

He also had to hope for a break soon, because they were running out of time. There were exactly two weeks left until September 1, and with every day that passed, Grant got more anxious.

Shana shrugged at his question, and Grant tried to imagine her the way she'd looked in the police file. Back then, she'd had long brown hair, blue eyes and a lean frame. Even though to him she hadn't really resembled Maggie, he had to admit the basics were the same. For a serial rapist, the women definitely fit a "type." Now they looked nothing alike.

Shana's overdyed hair hung around an unremarkable face, and she seemed wrung out, with none of the energy and determination that practically seeped from Maggie.

"Jeff was my ex. We'd broken up a few weeks before."

"The police report says you saw him that night? He was at the party?"

"Yeah, he showed up, begged me to take him back. I refused. Again. He left, I think with some other girl."

"You see him after that?" Grant asked.

"A couple of times. We actually got back together, real briefly, about six months later, but it didn't last long at all. Maybe a week or so."

"Why didn't it work?"

Her face twisted with distaste. "He was cocky, obnoxious. Rich-kid syndrome, my roommate called it. I'm not even sure why I went out with him in the first place, except he was cute."

"What about Kevin?"

Shana scowled. "*That* guy creeped me out. I tried to get a restraining order against him, but police said they needed some kind of threat or something first."

"He was stalking you?"

"Yeah. He was angry that I wouldn't go out with him. And his daddy was some kind of big deal, so he seemed to think if he bragged about that enough, I'd suddenly go out with him."

"Was he still hanging around after your attack?"

"Oh, yeah. He hung around until I graduated and moved away. Then I guess he moved on to someone else."

Grant looked up from jotting notes. "You know who?"

"No. I just assume he did. That's how those guys work, right?"

"Usually." Grant shut his notebook and gave her his full attention. "Anything else you can tell me about that night? Anything at all?"

"I told the police everything. Everything I could remember, anyway. I don't even know how I got the drugs. My drink, I guess, but I always got my own."

"At a frat party, it could have been in the keg, or with whoever was mixing drinks or—"

"Canned beer," Shana said. "That's what I was drinking. I wasn't stupid. Friend of mine had been dosed a few weeks before."

That was news to Grant. "What was her name? Did she file a report?"

"She didn't get raped. I was with her when she started feeling weird. We took her to the hospital."

"They figure out who drugged her?"

"No. It happened at another party. But she was drinking whatever was handed to her."

Grant frowned, wondering if there could be a connection, and wondering how Shana had been dosed. "Anyone else hold your beer for you?"

"I don't remember. It was more than a decade ago. I've been married, divorced, married again, and had two kids since then. Not to mention gotten my degree, worked for four different companies, lived in two other states before I came back here. I don't remember who might have held my drink thirteen years ago."

Grant nodded, not really surprised. "Have you seen Kevin or Jeff in the last ten years?"

"No." She studied him more intently. "What happened to me back then sucked, but how could it possibly be connected to a current case? I mean, it was probably some frat guy who took advantage of the fact that I was unconscious in his basement, right?"

"I'm just running a theory," Grant said, handing her his card. "But if you think of anything else, or if you have any other ideas about that day, can you give me a call?"

"Yeah, okay," Shana said. She tucked his card in her pocket, where Grant figured she'd forget about it within the hour, and probably toss it in the wash with her jeans. Without a backward glance, she disappeared inside.

Grant probably would have forgotten about most of his chat with Shana, too, except something nagged him until he got back to the office and opened Maggie's case file again. He skimmed over the details of what she remembered from her assault.

College party. She'd been there with friends and a boyfriend. Her friends had left early, then she'd fought with the boyfriend, so she'd headed back to the dorm alone. It was on that walk back when she'd been taken.

Grant kept reading, then his heart rate picked up when he read the details about her being drugged. The only thing she remembered drinking at the party was canned beer, beer she'd opened herself.

Just like Shana.

Chapter Eight

Maggie rubbed her eyes, trying to focus on the report she'd been filling out for the past few hours. She should have been able to knock it out in half an hour, but her vision kept going unfocused; her mind kept wandering to the Fishhook Rapist case, and then suddenly another hour had passed.

At least the office had mostly emptied out, and there weren't a lot of agents there to witness her struggling over simple paperwork. Her civil rights squad supervisor had finally left, after asking her no fewer than three times if she needed some time away.

She'd told him no just like she had last week, and last month, when he'd first learned about the letters. But if two more weeks passed and they still had no idea about the identity of the Fishhook Rapist, maybe she should do it. The FBI would offer her protection, of course, but maybe she should just take off, head somewhere far, far away.

Hide. Go to ground, and pray he wasn't savvy enough to follow.

Gritting her teeth, Maggie closed the file and turned off her desk light. As appealing as the idea sounded, she knew she'd never do it.

Because no matter how much the thought of facing

her attacker again terrified her, she wasn't twenty-two anymore. She wasn't drugged and helpless. If this guy really planned to come for her again, he'd be facing down a trained SWAT agent armed with every weapon the FBI had issued her.

And come September 1, there was no question she'd be surrounded by Ella and Scott like always. She suspected that Ella's fiancé, Logan, a seasoned police detective and Scott's girlfriend, Chelsie, an FBI negotiator, would be there, too. Knowing Grant, whether she asked him or not, he'd show up with a small arsenal and plant himself directly in front of her.

What chance did the Fishhook Rapist really have?

Maggie sighed, getting up from her desk. It didn't matter how much she told herself that; it didn't even matter how logical it was. Because every time she so much as thought about September 1, her hands started to shake.

Even the idea of walking into the parking garage right now—despite the fact that no one who didn't possess FBI credentials could get in there—made her irrationally nervous.

Get it together, she told herself.

Her phone trilled, and she jumped, instantly chastising herself for letting her fear override common sense. "Maggie Delacorte," she answered.

"Hey, Maggie, it's Nikki."

Nikki. Maggie closed her eyes and tried to make her voice cheery. She didn't want her little sister worrying about her. She'd tried hard for so long to keep this from touching Nikki, and she didn't plan to stop now. "How's the new apartment? And when do you start your job?"

"The apartment's great," Nikki said. "And I start in a few weeks. So I was thinking I have time to come and stay with you and Scott for a little bit. I figured maybe the three of us—and Ella, of course—could go out on September 1." Her voice turned hesitant. "You know, do something fun."

It was sweet of her sister, especially since the whole family babied her, and she probably could have gotten away with acting completely spoiled. But she never had.

Still, Maggie didn't want her anywhere near DC right now. She also didn't want her worrying. "That's nice of you, Nikki, but work is really busy right now. For Scott, too. The timing won't work, but I'm going to make a trip home next month. See your new place."

"Okay," Nikki said slowly. "Well, I would stay out of your way. I just thought—"

"Thank you. Really. But another time, okay?" Maggie said, knowing the strain was starting to come through in her voice.

"Okay," Nikki conceded. "Is everything all right?"

"Just busy," Maggie lied, and she had a feeling her sister could tell. "I'm actually still at work. Can I call you later?"

"Sure." Her sister sounded disappointed. "Let me know if you change your mind."

"I'll talk to you soon," Maggie said, feeling relieved as soon as she hung up the phone.

A hand clapped her on the shoulder as she put the phone in her purse, and she turned, startled.

"Sorry," Grant said, and put a steadying hand under her elbow.

"It's okay," Maggie said, easing her arm free. "I'm just a little jumpy tonight."

He frowned at her, looking worried, but all he said was, "Can I ask you some questions?"

"Okay." She studied him more closely, the dark circles under his eyes, the rolled-up sleeves on his dress shirt that showcased muscular forearms. Even though she was used to seeing him in his office clothes, he looked more natural in his SWAT getup. Maybe because he was built like a linebacker, khakis and a button-down never looked quite right on him.

Looking back to his face, she noticed the tight line of his lips, as if he was about to do something he didn't want to. "It's about the Fishhook Rapist case, isn't it?"

"Yeah. I'm sorry. I'm just trying—"

"No, it's fine." She tried to keep the exhaustion out of her own voice, knowing that Grant had been working more hours than anyone in the office since he'd been assigned to this case. Knowing that it was for her. "What is it?"

"The night you were drugged, your report says you were drinking beer out of a can. Is that right?"

Maggie gritted her teeth and nodded.

"Do you remember if you had anything else? Or if anyone could have—"

"You're wondering how I was drugged?" When he nodded, Maggie shook her head. "I'm not sure. Back then, I didn't know the things I do now, but I was relatively street smart. I didn't take drinks from people at parties, or let anyone I didn't know hang on to it, or leave it anywhere. I opened it myself. Best guess is that someone dropped the drugs in without me noticing."

Grant frowned. "Hmm. Okay. Are you sure no one got it for you?"

"Well, my boyfriend did, but I opened it."

"Do you know the names Jeff Hoffmeier or Kevin Sanders?"

"No. Why?"

He seemed disappointed, but not surprised, by her answer. "Just running some theories. Thanks."

As he turned to go back to the conference room, Maggie grabbed his arm and felt his muscles tense at her touch. "Are they suspects?"

"Not right now." She thought he was going to say more, but Kammy walked into the bullpen, her eyes narrowing when she saw them standing close together.

"Maggie," Kammy said, nodding at her, then she looked pointedly at Grant.

"Back to work it is. Thanks, Maggie."

When Kammy turned and headed off to the coffeepot, Maggie touched his arm again before he could follow. "Grant."

"Yeah?"

She stared up at him, not sure what she'd actually planned to say. She saw him in the office every day, but lately it had felt different. Even standing in front of him now, doing something as impersonal as touching his forearm, felt intimate.

She had a sudden flashback to the feel of his hands clutching her thighs as he lifted her onto his lap, the feel of his body pressed tight to hers, his heartbeat thundering against her palm. Heat spread through her.

It must have shown on her face, because his pupils suddenly dilated as he stared back at her.

Her voice came out huskier than usual when she blurted, "Uh, why don't you come over after you finish here? We can talk."

"Sure," he said, sounding surprised. He glanced at his watch, and when he looked up at her again, there was anticipation in his eyes. "Probably an hour or two?"

"Whenever," she said, then watched him hurry back to the conference room, knowing he'd thought she wanted to talk about what had happened between them last night. Or maybe start right back up where they'd left off.

She tried not to feel guilty as she walked to the parking garage. Because he was in for quite a surprise when he did arrive at her house, and that's not what she was after at all.

WHEN IT CAME to work, Grant had never been able to do anything but go all-in. He couldn't help himself. With his cases, it was all or nothing. It had gotten him in trouble a time or two, namely during the Manhattan Strangler case.

If he'd waited for backup the way he'd been told to, he probably wouldn't have ended up in the hospital getting stitches for a nasty stab wound. He wouldn't have ended up with the censure in his Bureau file, or ultimately decided it was time to transfer to a new field office for a fresh start.

Then again, if he'd waited for backup, the victim surely would have died. And the Manhattan Strangler probably would have gotten away yet again.

So he'd never been able to regret his actions. Not on that case, and not on any job where he went in strong, the way SWAT let him do as their designated door-kicker.

But in his personal life, he was a little more restrained, particularly when it came to relationships. He'd had a few that had approached serious, but he'd never felt that all-consuming need to dive in, the way he did with his cases. Not until Maggie.

Which was probably why he was standing on her doorstep right now, instead of home in bed. Because she might have been purposely vague about why she wanted to talk to him tonight, but he'd realized exactly why she'd invited him over.

She wanted to grill him for details about the case. Details he was supposed to keep confidential.

Swearing, Grant lowered his fist from the door instead

of knocking, but it opened, anyway. And suddenly the cars in the driveway made sense, because it wasn't Maggie who answered, but her friend Ella Cortez.

A feisty profiler in the Bureau's Behavioral Analysis Unit, who'd shown up with Maggie a few times at O'Reilley's. He didn't know her particularly well, but he'd seen her name in Maggie's police file from a decade ago. Ella was one of the friends who'd left the party, thinking Maggie was safe with her boyfriend. She'd been the one to call the police the next morning when Maggie had stumbled back to their shared dorm room, bleeding and branded on the back of the neck.

"Ella, hi," he said.

It almost seemed that she could read what he was thinking, but she just said evenly, "Grant."

Then she stepped backward and led him toward the living room, where Grant saw a group of people gathered. "Come on in. We've been waiting for you."

His eyebrows rose. "I didn't realize it was going to be a party."

"Sorry about that," Maggie said as she came toward him, dodging an open pizza box on the floor.

She'd changed out of the dress pants and stiff, short-sleeved blouse she'd worn at the office into curve-hugging jeans and a well-worn T-shirt that looked more *Maggie*. His fingers itched to touch the soft cotton, to caress the skin underneath.

As he stared at her, probably broadcasting his every thought for the entire room, she lowered her voice. "I figured if I told you—"

"I knew what you wanted to talk about." He was trying to stop staring at those gorgeous blue eyes of hers, but ever since he'd realized her attraction to him might actually come close to how he felt for her, he seemed to have lost all his willpower. "I just didn't realize you ex-pected me to break protocol in front of a crowd."

She turned red, but Scott came up behind her and said, "You don't have to worry about that. Nothing you say leaves this room."

The serious, massively protective, big-brother expres-sion on Scott's face made Grant get his act together. He stood a little straighter and ripped his attention away from Maggie. "Quid pro quo?"

"Absolutely," Scott answered. "We'll share everything we're thinking. But I've got to tell you, it isn't much. We don't have the access you do. But you know we're not going to sit idly by on this one."

"Neither will I," Grant said, and he knew his conviction—and probably the strength of his feelings for Maggie—rang in those words. "I'll do whatever it takes to get this guy."

Scott stared back at him a minute, then simply nod-ded, but Grant could see in that minute he'd won Scott's approval.

"Let's get going, then," Scott said.

Ella had already sat down in a chair in the corner, be-side a guy who looked about Grant's age. He had gruff, hard features, dark, close-cropped hair and the intuitive stare that immediately labeled him as law enforcement.

"Logan Greer." The man stood and introduced him-self with a hint of a drawl. "I'm Ella's fiancé and a de-tective with the DC PD."

"Nice to meet you," Grant said.

"Hi, Grant," the last person in the room called from the floor, where she was jotting notes in a legal file with one hand and holding a slice of pizza in the other.

"Chelsie," he replied. Chelsie Russell was a willowy blonde who worked in the WFO and had an ancillary position as a negotiator. When he'd first met her, she'd seemed stiff and quiet, but she and Maggie were friends, so he'd learned she actually had a pretty good sense of humor and a decent break at the pool table.

"So we've got a couple of tactical agents, a profiler, a negotiator and a detective," Grant summed up. Not to mention his experience on the violent crimes division and Maggie's work in civil rights cases. "Let's see what we can come up with here."

He tried to ignore the voice buzzing in the back of his brain telling him this was going to end like the Manhattan Strangler case, with yet another censure in his file for disobeying orders.

He glanced at Maggie and found her looking gratefully at him. Suddenly, he didn't care what the case did to his file, so long as the other part of the Manhattan Strangler case didn't come back to haunt him. Because he couldn't bear to watch Maggie get hurt.

Just the thought of it made his chest tense up until his breathing felt unnatural.

Forcing himself to focus, he found a spot on the floor, helped himself to a slice of pizza and told the group the details of the Shana Mills case. "She didn't show up at the hospital until September 2, but she was assaulted on the first, thirteen years ago."

"Okay." Scott sounded skeptical. "What happened in the two years in between, then? Other victims who he didn't brand? On the same date?"

"Maybe, but none of the other cases I looked at had any similarities. And if there was no branding, I'm not sure the date matters."

Ella started shaking her head and leaned forward, so Grant cut her off. "Look, I'm no profiler, but the date is significant for a reason, right? Don't you think there's a good chance it was the date he assaulted the person he actually *knew*, the one he really wanted to hurt? Originally?"

Ella frowned, grooves appearing between her eyebrows. "My theory is that the date is important because it's when he finally took the step he'd fantasized about for years. It's when he finally abducted someone, and everything that came after that. And he wanted to keep doing it. That's why he's coming back for her. Ten years have gone by. Ten years to build up the sick obsession of his first target. Ten years, and suddenly he's not having such an easy time fitting in around these college students. He's looking for a replay of when it all worked for him."

Her voice was strained, and as her fiancé put his arm around Ella's shoulders, Grant realized how hard it was for her to profile Maggie's case.

"I think you're wrong."

Everyone stilled and stared back at him at the announcement, probably because Ella was a heck of a profiler. Even he knew it, and he'd never worked with her.

"You were there when it happened. You're too close to see it clearly."

She jerked back as though she'd been insulted, and he quickly added, "I'm sorry. I just think the date has to be more significant. Otherwise, why wait so long? If it was really just about when he started, why not make it the first of every month? Or every six months? There's still a pattern in that, and then he's not forced to wait a whole *year*. It's got to be more. It's got to be *personal*."

Silence greeted his argument, and Grant cursed himself for his word choice. The September 1 a decade ago was extremely personal to everyone in this room.

It was Chelsie who finally spoke up. "Why this case? Why Shana Mills?"

"She's pretty sure someone drugged the beer she was drinking. Beer in a can, that she opened herself."

"So what?" Ella said, then held up a hand when he started to continue. "Yeah, I know that's what happened to Maggie, but what does that tell us? That both perps were savvy enough to get close to their victims without being noticed. Doesn't make it the same person."

She was right, but something about this file brought his investigative instincts to life.

"Then there's this." He handed Ella the copy of Shana Mills's picture he'd taken from the case file.

Her eyes went from the picture to him and back again. "Okay," she admitted, "there's a certain type here. Same basic look as all the Fishhook victims."

Maggie, who'd been mostly silent and still during the exchange, reached over from where she'd been standing, arms crossed in the corner, and took the picture. She frowned. "You think she looks like me?"

The truth was, he didn't. Not in the ways that mattered. But when it came to the basics—the long, dark hair with the off-center part, the light blue eyes, the slender, toned figure—the similarities were definitely there.

"It's a type," Ella spoke up. "The kind of similarities this guy might be looking for." She looked at Grant. "It's still not a sure thing. Scott's right about the two-year wait."

"You think he would have started the branding the very next year, if my theory is right?" Grant pressed, genuinely wanting Ella's opinion. She knew this kind of killer better than he ever would, regardless of how close she was to the case.

She fiddled with the diamond on her finger, seeming to have an internal argument, before she finally said, "Not necessarily. You could be right about there being more victims who weren't branded in between, and then the date might not be as important. Or it's possible he waited, put together his plan, found a location, did practice runs."

"Practice runs?" Logan asked, sounding as if he wasn't sure he wanted to know what that meant.

"Victims he killed. Or victims he didn't think would ever report, even with a brand. Prostitutes, for example."

"So what do we do with this?" Scott was tapping his foot incessantly, which made him seem desperate to move, and move now.

"It's just a theory," Grant said. "Two names came up in Shana's file. I'm going to run them down."

"Jeff Hoffmeier and Kevin Sanders," Maggie said.

"Yeah." He squinted at her, surprised she'd remembered the names he'd mentioned at the office. "*I'm* going to run this down," he emphasized. "If it leads anywhere, I'll loop you in."

Maggie looked as if she was going to argue, but Scott cut her off. "We're trying to go at this from the traveling angle. How does he move around so much, and what does that mean for his occupation? We're considering trucker, contractor, independently wealthy—"

"Wealthy," Grant interrupted. "The marble table."

"What marble table?" Chelsie asked, setting her pen down and staring up at him.

Grant swore as he looked over at Maggie, then started to apologize.

"It's fine," she said. "I haven't had a chance to tell them all the details. I had a flashback. I remembered room details. I wasn't thinking about what it meant for the profile, but the room I was in was nice. It wasn't some dive hotel. It was someone's house."

Ella stood. "Maggie, that's huge. That means he *did* live here ten years ago. When he talked about *home* in his letter, it wasn't a figure of speech. We need to start looking at anyone who lived on or around campus back then who moved within the year."

Maggie sighed loudly. "That's been done several times over the years. Besides, the number will be huge. With all the colleges around here, the population shift is enormous. And if he left in the summer right before the following September, it would be when a whole graduating class left."

"Yeah, but he was older," Ella said. "He wasn't a college student. That I'd bank on. Although…"

"What?" Scott demanded.

Ella looked at Grant. "If you're right about Shana Mills, he could have been a student *then*. Probably not an undergrad, but maybe a grad student or a teaching assistant or something."

"Okay." Grant's energy level, which had been hovering around zero when he'd arrived, suddenly spiked. This was the best lead he'd had yet. And if it wasn't the ex-boyfriend or the stalker, it was probably someone in Shana's life. Someone who'd been in DC thirteen years ago, and who'd been here ten years ago, but had left sometime after September 1 of that year.

Even though he didn't have any solid evidence to back up the connection to Shana Mills, he knew he was onto something.

He glanced at his watch—9:30 p.m. Kammy would probably still be at the office. "I need to go. Let me know if you come up with anything. And I'll tell you what happens on my end with the interviews of those two guys."

Maggie nodded, but there was something in her expression…

Grant looked at Scott. "Can I talk to you in private for a second?"

Maggie didn't seem happy about that, but Scott nodded. "Yeah, okay."

"I'll be in touch," he promised everyone as he followed Scott down the hall and to the front entryway, where there was a modicum of privacy.

"We're sticking close," Scott told him before he could say a word.

"Good." Grant pulled a card out of his pocket and handed it over. "Just call me if you need help. I'll be here. The same is true of any of the guys on the team. They all love your sister."

As soon as the words were out of his mouth, Grant felt as if someone had sucker punched him.

"You okay, man?" Scott asked.

"Yeah, fine." He tried to shake off the realization that had just hit him, but the knowledge rattled around in his brain even as he tried to focus. "Look, this perp knows Maggie is SWAT. He must."

"Which makes him an idiot," Scott spat. "I mean, believe me, I'm not leaving her alone, but she doesn't need me. You should know—you see her working on SWAT."

"That's the thing," Grant countered. "He's *not* an idiot. He has to be really intelligent to have pulled this off for a decade."

"So you're thinking, what? That he doesn't actually plan to get close again? You thinking a long-distance shooting?"

Grant swore at that idea, which had never occurred to him. "No. Talk to Ella, because she knows this stuff better, but I don't think so. But he's *obsessed* with Maggie, fixated on her in a way he's never been on any of the others. So he must have a plan to get near her. Unless maybe his plan is purely psychological? Break her down by giving her reason to believe he's coming after her, then stick to his normal pattern and grab someone else?"

Scott nodded, looking grim. "Well, we're going to assume he's serious. But you could be right. Every year, waiting for a new report…" Scott shook his head. "It's really hard on her. If she's focused on this threat against her, and that's where the manpower is, and then he hurts some other woman…"

"I know."

"Thanks for helping out," Scott said.

"Of course."

Scott slapped his arm and walked back toward the living room, his steps slow, as if he didn't want to talk to Maggie about the possibilities Grant had suggested.

Grant stepped outside but before he'd made it off the stoop, Maggie ran out, closing the door behind her.

"I just told your brother—"

"To keep an eye on me," Maggie said, interrupting him. "I get it. Look…" She trailed off, studying him. "Are you okay?"

A smile slipped out as he stared back at her. "Yeah, I'm okay." He stepped forward, until they were standing close to each other.

He didn't know how deep her feelings for him ran. She was attracted to him, and they were friends, and at least to some extent, she was using his feelings for her to get his help on this case. But was there more?

He lifted his hand, stroked the side of her cheek, and she leaned her face into his palm. He moved a little closer, until he could feel her breath on his chin. Until he could lower his lips and press them lightly to hers, try to show her what he'd realized, what he wasn't ready to say out loud.

He was in love with her.

Chapter Nine

When Maggie walked back into her living room, everyone was staring at her. Everyone but Logan, who was staring resolutely at the wall, obviously wanting no part of whatever was about to happen.

"What?" she demanded.

"What's the deal with Grant?" Ella asked, a smirk on her face that Maggie recognized all too well.

"Nothing," Maggie answered, knowing her voice was giving her away. "We're friends. You know that."

"I also know when you're lying to me," Ella answered, still looking smug. "I've known you way too long. You really think you can keep secrets from me?"

"I like him," Scott put in, and Maggie gaped at him.

"What? I do."

Over the years, Scott had taken his big-brother role with both her and Ella a little too seriously, especially when it came to guys, and even more so since her attack. He'd gone easier on Ella, and he'd approved of Logan, but Maggie didn't think anyone had ever passed his test for her.

"Well, that doesn't matter," she started, but Ella cut her off.

"I wondered how long that was going to take."

"What are you talking about?"

Ella leaned forward, grinning, and in the chair beside her, Logan made "sorry my fiancée is nosy" gestures so animated that Maggie couldn't help but laugh.

Ella glared briefly at him, then continued, "The times you invited me along with your SWAT team to O'Reilley's, I could tell you were interested. And so was he." She looked pleased with herself when she added, "I wondered how long it would take for you two to finally admit it."

"Well, it doesn't matter," Maggie said again, settling back on the couch beside her brother and crossing her arms over her chest to signal that the discussion was over.

"Why? Because he's a teammate?" Chelsie asked.

"He's not a teammate anymore," Maggie said, and stopped Scott before he could jump in as she knew he wanted to, telling her she'd get back on SWAT. She definitely didn't want to get into that discussion. "Grant's investigating my case, so that's the end of it."

"He's trying—" Ella started.

"I don't want to talk about it," Maggie blurted, and her friends went silent, because she rarely refused to discuss anything. "It's not happening, so just leave it alone."

Scott and Ella shared a glance that Maggie purposely ignored, and then Logan spoke up, clearly trying to change the subject. "Look, this isn't my specialty, but given what Grant was suggesting about that Shana Mills case, if the perp actually knew her, is there any chance he knew Maggie, too?"

Ella sat straighter beside him, instantly serious, and started shaking her head, then paused, looking pensive. "He wouldn't have been someone in Maggie's life. But if she was the first one he didn't know, it was a change in tactics, so it's possible he was around the periphery."

"What do you mean?" Scott demanded, leaning forward, the muscles in his arms bulging.

Ella looked at Maggie. "The thing Grant said about your drink. We know this guy stalked you. He would have done that with all of his victims. If he got close enough to slip drugs into your drink while you were holding it, maybe he talked to you. Maybe you knew him in some way—not well, maybe not even well enough to know his name, but enough to recognize him when he walked past you."

Numbness started to fill Maggie, and she recognized it as the coping mechanism she'd adopted whenever the discussions turned to areas she didn't like. Usually it happened when talking to investigators about specific details, not with her friends. But the idea that she might have known the person who had hurt her, even in some small way?

The numbness evaporated, and cold swept over her in its place, a light-headed feeling she tried to replace with anger. "So you think I could recognize him now?" she asked, and her voice sounded as though it was coming from far away.

Concern wrinkled Ella's face, but she nodded. "It's possible. I think you should ask Grant to take a look at pictures of any of his suspects."

Maggie nodded, even as discomfort overwhelmed her. It was bad enough that Grant was investigating, and hard enough to discuss the case with him—as though it didn't hurt her to think about him digging into the worst day of her life. She really didn't want to dig through it with him.

But if it meant catching the Fishhook Rapist, she'd do it. Because no matter how hard she tried not to dwell on it, she knew exactly how long she had left. Thirteen days, two hours and six minutes until it hit September 1.

And then the Fishhook Rapist would be back for her.

MAGGIE COULDN'T WAIT any longer.

She'd been sitting at her desk, staring at her files, for over an hour, waiting for Kammy Ming to finally call it quits and head home. So she could talk to Grant alone. But the WFO had pretty well cleared out, and Grant and Kammy were still cloistered in the conference room, going over the case.

Her stomach rolling at the idea of what she was about to do, Maggie stood, moving through the dark and empty bullpen toward the conference room fast, before she could back out.

When she opened the door, Grant and Kammy stared back at her with surprise. They were sitting across from each other at a long conference table that was covered in open case files, boxes and laptops. A whiteboard at the far end of the room was inked up with notes, and a map pinned next to it had red circles and writing that Maggie didn't need to get close to to read. She recognized the locations instantly. The nine credited attacks of the Fishhook Rapist, scattered across the country.

She tried not to look at the files as she headed for the far end of the room where Grant and Kammy sat. Grant stood as she approached, and she couldn't help herself from glancing over the contents on the table. A box full of information on the fishing industry. Stacks of college attendance records from all across DC from a decade ago. Victim case files.

Over the years, Maggie had been tempted to try and reach out to the other victims, try to piece together what they knew. Try to get answers. But she'd resisted. Not just because it would have been completely against protocol, but also because she didn't want to go over every tiny, insignificant thing she could remember, or the big hole in her memory. So how could she ask someone else to do it?

As she reached Grant's side, Maggie forced herself to look away from the case files before she spotted her own. She knew what was in it, and she didn't want or need to see it. She had enough memories.

"We're doing everything we can," Kammy told her, sounding worn-out, and beneath the seasoned investigator's voice was something that sounded an awful lot like defeat.

"What is it, Maggie?" Grant asked, as he closed the file next to him, which had to be hers.

She tried to keep the emotion out of her voice as she told him, "I want to look at pictures."

"What pictures?" Grant asked, just as Kammy said, "You need to leave the investigation to us."

How was she going to do this without letting Kammy know Grant had been sharing information with her? Frustration filled her, because she couldn't wait around to talk to Grant in secret. Keeping her personal investigation segregated from their official one was limiting resources. What if not working together prevented them from finding the Fishhook Rapist in time?

"If there's a chance this guy started with someone he knew before me, maybe he hung around me when he was stalking me. Maybe I could recognize him."

Kammy glared at Grant. "I know James talked to you about confidentiality—"

"It's not him," Maggie said. "I'm an agent, too. I can't sit back and leave this to someone else. I'm looking into it myself."

For a split second, Kammy looked furious, but Maggie

could see her making a concerted effort to rein it in as she said, "There's a reason you weren't assigned this case, Maggie. You're too close to it, and you know it."

"I can help," Maggie snapped. "I want to look at the pictures. I don't want to be sitting in my house, hoping this guy won't come back for me in thirteen days, because you were worried about bureaucratic procedure!"

Kammy stood, and even though Maggie had eight inches and probably thirty pounds on her, she suddenly understood why Kammy had a reputation as someone not to cross. The full force of her glare was intimidating.

But Maggie was SWAT—or at least she had been—and she glared right back.

Grant held his hands out and said calmly, "Look, this is on me. I told Maggie my theory. I asked if she recognized the names from the Mills file. No sense in spreading our resources thin if she knew them. She didn't, but let's see if the faces ring any bells. Okay?"

Kammy turned on Grant again and gave one curt nod, and Maggie knew her outburst had just put a dent, not in her career, but Grant's.

Ashamed, she opened her mouth to apologize, but Grant held out a file before she could speak.

"Here," he said. "This is the stalker, Kevin Sanders. He look familiar?"

Her hands shook as she took the file from him, and she braced herself. But when she stared at the picture of Kevin Sanders from thirteen years ago—blond hair, cocky smile, college sweatshirt even though he'd already graduated—she felt nothing. No sudden burst of recognition, no painful memories. Nothing.

She looked harder, willing something forward. They already knew he was a stalker, and if Shana Mills was the original victim, he had to be first in the suspect line. If it was him, they would have a name, a person to hunt down.

Finally, she looked up at Grant and shook her head. "I don't recognize him."

"That's okay." Grant closed the file and set it down. "We're still going to check him out." He handed her a second file. "The ex-boyfriend, Jeff Hoffmeier."

She opened it fast, expecting nothing, but hoping for... something. But just like Kevin Sanders, he didn't look familiar. He was scowling slightly, which made what would have otherwise been a good-looking face seem ugly and angry. His dark hair was buzzed close to his head, and his eyes were strikingly blue. He had apparently already graduated a few years earlier when he'd been dating Shana, but he still looked like a college kid in the picture. A typical college kid.

She started to shake her head and hand back the file when a voice from her past whispered in her head, *What are you drinking?* The same voice that she remembered from one other time, telling her, *This is going to hurt*.

She gasped, and the file slipped from her hands, spilling its contents all over the floor.

"Hey." Grant's hand locked on her arm, and the voice in her mind faded. "You recognize this guy?"

Kammy leaned toward them across the table, looking expectant, a phone already in her hand, as if she was ready to call in the rest of the team.

"Uh, I don't know." Her voice shook, and Maggie tried to get it together. She reached down for the file, and Grant stopped her.

"I got it." He set the file on the table. "Did he look familiar?"

"Let me look again."

"You want to take a break?"

"No, I'm fine." She gritted her teeth and opened the file on the table, taking out just the picture. She focused hard, studying Jeff Hoffmeier more closely.

He had a strong, angular face, an aristocratic nose and a strong jawline. He'd probably had an easy time getting dates, if he didn't scowl the way he was doing in the picture. But no matter how intently she stared at him, willing the memory back, she didn't recognize him.

So why had that memory rushed forward when she'd looked at his picture?

Was it even a real memory? She had no recollection of the Fishhook Rapist ever talking to her before the abduction, no recollection of him asking her about her drink, even though he'd obviously dosed it. Had the investigation created false memories?

She knew it could happen. She'd seen it firsthand in her own cases. The further back an incident was, the harder the memories were to access. The more details a victim had about the possible suspects, the more likely she was to talk herself into believing something just because she needed answers.

Was the same true of Maggie, despite her FBI training?

"Do you know him?" Kammy asked, and Grant said, "Give her a second." Their voices seemed distant as she kept staring desperately at Jeff Hoffmeier.

Finally, she set the image down and shook her head. "I'm not sure. He gives me a bad feeling, but he doesn't look familiar."

"What does that mean?" Kammy asked, sounding frustrated. "You think this is him or not?"

Grant glared at Kammy, but when he turned back to her, his expression was even and calm. "What about him gives you a bad feeling?"

"I'm not sure. I think I had a memory when I looked at his picture, but it was just a voice. And I can't be certain…" She sighed heavily, infuriated that she couldn't say more. She'd always been grateful that she couldn't remember much from the attack itself, but suddenly she wished she did.

"I'm not sure *why* that happened. Maybe it's him, or maybe something about him just reminds me of the guy. I don't know." She heard the anguished frustration in her voice and tried to even it out, like the professional she was. "Maybe when you talk to this guy, I should go with you."

"No," Grant barked.

"If it's him, and he sees me, he might—"

"No," Grant cut her off. "We'll look into him more closely, see if he's even a possibility. If he looks good for it, we'll bring him in, and if there's a reason for you to get involved, you can do it through the glass."

"That's not—"

"It's not happening," Kammy said softly, and Grant looked as though he might burst an artery.

"Okay, look—"

"We're not tipping our hand on this." Grant seemed to be working hard to keep his voice calm. "Once we narrow in on a name, there's going to be a pattern, and it might take a little time to dig up, but it will be there. We're not letting anyone know they're on our suspect list until we show up at their door to slap the cuffs on, got it?"

Maggie frowned, unable to deny the logic there. She definitely didn't want him running, if it was him. "Okay, then why haven't you started digging into information on these two already?" They had to be at the top of the list, if Grant's theory was to be believed. "I can—"

"We had some other leads today that looked good," Kammy said. "But they didn't pan out."

"What were they?"

"They didn't pan out," Kammy repeated tightly. "But Grant is right. If Hoffmeier is the guy, then he's lived in all the locations on the board." She gestured vaguely behind her at the map with the bright red circles. "And we'll find that."

Maggie nodded. Their plan made sense. "Okay." She pushed a stack of files aside and settled into the chair next to where Grant had been sitting until she walked into the room. "I'll help."

"No way," Kammy burst out.

Maggie crossed her arms over her chest and gave Kammy her best SWAT stare, the one that said she wasn't backing down. "You want me out of here, you're going to have to drag me. And I've got to warn you, you're not going to have an easy time of it."

"Are you kidding me?" Kammy let out a stream of curses more creative than Maggie thought the uptight woman knew.

"I'll track locations," Maggie insisted as she tried not to look at Grant. She could see him out of the corner of her eye, staring at her with an expression she couldn't quite read.

Anger? Worry? Disappointment? Probably all three, and she didn't want to think about what her actions were doing to his reputation within VCMO, or how they were going to impact his feelings for her.

"Fine," Kammy said tightly. "But you research what we hand over, and nothing else. Any more than that, and I don't care about your personal stake in this. The rules exist for a reason, and you step any further over the line, and I'm putting it in both of your files. Got it?"

Maggie nodded, the fear of harming Grant's career weighing on her more than the chances of hurting her own. And from the perceptive look in Kammy's eyes, she knew it.

"You take Sanders," Grant said, handing her the file.

"I want—"

"I'll deal with Hoffmeier," Grant interrupted. "Kammy was already digging into other people in Shana's life who might be involved."

Maggie looked up at her, where she was still standing, looking irate. "You find anyone?"

"No." She dropped into her seat, wrestled her jet-black hair streaked with gray into a knot and added, "I'm still looking, though."

"Thank you."

Kammy frowned at her. "I respect your work here, Maggie, or I wouldn't let this—" she gestured around her at the files "—slide. But watch your step. If you want to be involved with this in any capacity, you need to stop your side investigation. I don't want you running across this guy unprepared."

Maggie nodded, hoping she looked convincing. Kammy's argument was logical, but no way were Ella or her brother stopping, which meant she wasn't, either.

Kammy's eyes narrowed suspiciously, so Maggie grabbed the Kevin Sanders file and started working.

It didn't take long before her heart rate picked up, and she began to wonder whether her reaction to Jeff had actually been a delayed response to seeing Kevin Sanders's picture. He'd served two stints in jail in the past five years, both for sexual assault.

Neither were in states where Fishhook Rapist victims had appeared, but they were in between attacks, so they could have been en route to a new state. She sat straighter, sifting through information faster, looking for a connection.

An hour later, she sank back in her seat and shook her head, trying not to dwell on her disappointment. "It's not Kevin Sanders."

Grant looked up from his own laptop and rubbed his eyes. "Why not?"

The dejection sounded in her voice when she told him and Kammy, "At the time of the third victim's attack, he was in lockup for drunk driving. Thirty days. There's no way it was him."

"I haven't come up with any other likely possibilities from Shana Mills's life," Kammy said, slumping back against her chair. "How's your luck, Grant?"

Maggie turned toward him expectantly, but one glance at the weary slump of his shoulders and her hope for a break in the case faded, especially as he shook his head.

"Jeff Hoffmeier is a real possibility."

"What?" Maggie sat straighter, grasping his arm before she realized what she was doing. She quickly pulled her hand back. "What do you mean?"

"He was living in DC ten years ago. After that, I have no idea."

Maggie frowned. "You can't track him? He has to have owned property, or gotten a driver's license or—"

"I can't track him," Grant said. "It's as if he just disappeared. And it happened sometime after September, ten years ago."

Chapter Ten

Grant had finally lain down in bed when the doorbell rang. He stared up at the ceiling in the darkness, sighed, then threw on a T-shirt and went to the door, feeling every step. It had been a very long, frustrating day, and the verbal warning from James—who'd had a call from Kammy about him and Maggie—had capped it off.

He opened the door, already knowing who was standing on the other side, and turned around, telling her, "Come on in."

"I'm sorry—"

"Stop apologizing," he told Maggie as he led her to the living room, squinting as he flipped on a light.

He turned around and faced her, discovering that she looked more worn out than he felt.

"I didn't mean to wake you. I just wanted to apolo—"

"Maggie," he said. "If you're going to start every visit to my house with an apology, it's going to get old fast. You want to come by, then come by because we're friends, and you want to see me. Come by because we're—" he paused, then settled on "—more than that, and you just want me." He grinned to let her know he was at least partly teasing, and finished, "Just don't say *sorry* one more time."

She fiddled with the hem of her blouse, stuck her hands in her pockets, took them out again and crossed them over her chest. "Okay. Sure." She glanced over his T-shirt and boxers, and added, "I didn't think you'd be sleeping."

It was still early evening, but he'd put in so many late nights during that past two weeks, he'd finally crashed.

"Long day," he said, settling onto the couch and gesturing for her to join him. "You're here to find out where we are on the case, I assume." He'd leaned his head against the back of the couch and closed his eyes, so he didn't know if she nodded or not as he felt her sit down next to him, but he continued, "Jeff Hoffmeier's name pops up a few times, but it's sporadic, and it's not giving us places of residence."

"What about his family? They're still in town."

Slowly, Grant opened his eyes and looked at her. She'd sat closer than he'd realized, and he could see the strain on her face that got worse with each day closer to September 1.

"I thought you were going to stay away from this." That had been their agreement, after she'd helped them the night before at the office. Kammy had insisted she stay away from Hoffmeier, and she'd agreed. Grant had known she wouldn't stay away from the investigation entirely, but he'd thought she'd conceded to focus on her safety, and let them run down the lead. Apparently, he'd been wrong.

Before she could reply, he swore. "Maggie, please tell me you didn't talk to them."

"I didn't give my name. I called, claimed to be from the alumni association, asked for contact information for him."

Grant sat up, suddenly wide-awake and furious. "Are you kidding me? Are you trying to sabotage this investigation?"

She leaned toward him until they were mere inches apart, looking furious herself. "You know me. You know I wasn't going to leave this to anyone else."

"I was checking into Hoffmeier," he growled. "I told you to leave it alone."

"Yeah, well, you're not my boss."

"Your boss told you to leave it alone, too."

"Too bad," she said. "I called. It's done. And they gave me the runaround, said he wouldn't want to be in the directory listing, even when I pushed for just a phone number to ask him myself."

Grant rubbed his forehead, where a headache was rapidly forming. "You're going to get yourself hurt," he said quietly, trying to keep the anger out of his voice. And he was successful. Because what came through was worry.

He felt her hand close on his, and even though he'd seen up close in SWAT what she was capable of doing with those hands, all he could focus on was how tiny they were, compared to his.

"I didn't go anywhere near him, and I don't plan to, even if I'd learned where he was. I made a phone call. If anything had come of it, I would have…"

"What?" he pressed when she paused. "Called Scott and taken him over there?"

"No," she replied. "I would have called you. I understand that I have a target on my back. I'm not going to put anyone else in danger by going near a possible suspect who's out to get me, and probably willing to take other people down to get to me. But that doesn't mean I'm going to sit home, boarding up my windows and praying someone else finds him, after a decade of dead ends. Come on!"

Grant tried to forcibly keep the words in that wanted to burst from his mouth. When he felt he had it together, he told her, "I'll pay the family a visit tomorrow."

"What about not tipping your hand?"

"If Hoffmeier is living in DC right now, he doesn't have his name on any lease. Which means he's either off the books somewhere, or his family is putting him up. They've got some serious political connections, and they're not going to scare easily, but they're also not going to want bad press attached to the family name. I'm going to use that."

"How?"

"Maggie, trust me, okay? I've run a lot of investigations like this. I understand why you can't back away, but just let me run with Hoffmeier."

"We've got twelve days, Grant," she said softly, nervousness in her eyes that he hadn't seen on even the diciest of SWAT calls.

He stroked her hand. "If we don't have someone in custody by August 31, the FBI is putting you in protective custody. And I'm taking a break from the case to be on the detail." That last part hadn't been approved, but it didn't matter. Whatever it took, he planned to be there for her.

She gave him a forced smile. "That's sweet of you, Grant, but I've got SWAT training. If he gets anywhere near me…"

"I know." He made sure he put conviction in the words, wanted her to know he believed them. "But this guy is smart, and I'm not willing to take chances. Neither is anyone in the Bureau. I didn't even need to request this. The word came down from way above me."

She was silent a minute, and he wasn't sure if she was digesting that, or trying to come up with an argument, but he spoke up first.

"Even if it wasn't an official order, Maggie, you know every single guy on our team would have taken personal time to stand by you on September 1. This SOB would have had to go through an entire team of SWAT agents to get anywhere near you."

Tears welled in her eyes—something he'd never once seen—and he finished, "But it's not going to come to that. We're going to get him."

She nodded. Then she reached up and put her hand on the back of his head to pull him to her, and softly kissed him. She leaned back again before he'd really registered what was happening. "Thank you."

She'd never let go of his hand, so he used it to tug her closer, until he could wrap his arm around her shoulder. He knew she cared about him, and she was attracted to him, but beyond that? He really had no idea. And now was the wrong time to find out, but when she rested her head in the crook of his arm and relaxed against him, it felt right, like something a girlfriend would do.

"When I was a teenager, my dad left."

Maggie shifted, apparently surprised by the change in conversation, but he kept his arm around her shoulder and drew her back against him.

"It was sort of out of the blue for all of us. My parents never had the most solid marriage, but they never argued, either. There was just this…distance. Then my dad just left. Middle of the night and everything. Packed up one suitcase and bolted. Left everything else behind, including his family."

Maggie's fingers tightened around his, telling him

she was listening carefully, even though he couldn't see her expression.

"I get postcards and phone calls every so often, but for all real purposes, he just washed his hands of us. Never got an explanation, either. I think that's the part that eats my mom up most. But the timing…" He sighed, remembering the changes that had come swift and unforgiving during his sophomore year of high school.

"We lived in the city. New York. We were already struggling, but without the second income, we had to move, and where we ended up was bad. Real bad. With a big gang presence."

"And they took one look at you and wanted you to join," Maggie guessed, reminding him she'd seen the picture on his mantel.

Even in high school, he'd looked like the kind of muscle a gang might want to use. "Yeah. My younger brothers weren't quite my size, but they tried to jump all three of us in. I worked hard to keep us all out of it."

"And what happened?"

The memory made him tense. "Vinnie was okay. It wasn't easy, but he genuinely wanted nothing to do with it, so even though it wasn't exactly simple to keep them off our doorstep, at least we were only fighting on one side there. But Ben—he's the baby of the family, in seventh grade then—he was interested. I honestly thought we were going to lose him to them. I'd all but given up, when one of his friends was killed in a drive-by. It scared him straight."

"They seem to be doing pretty well now," she said. "From your pictures, I mean."

"Oh, yeah. Vinnie's still in New York, but way up north now, and Ben moved out to Chicago a couple of years back."

"And you stayed in New York."

"Well, that's where the Bureau assigned me."

She twisted to look at him. "You requested it, though, didn't you? As your office of preference?"

Once an agent made it through the FBI Academy, they got to request the field office where they wanted to be placed. It was considered sort of a joke, because rarely did anyone seem to actually get their office of preference, but he had. "Yeah. Well, at the time, my family was still there, and I wanted to…"

"Make a difference," she finished.

"Sounds a little corny, I know, but—"

"It doesn't sound corny at all," she said.

"Well, I didn't get gangs, which honestly, I'm kind of glad about—I'd had plenty of that—but I've been in VCMO my whole career so far. I wanted to try for SWAT in New York, but there was never an opening. So when I came here and a place opened up right away, it seemed like it was meant to be."

"Maybe it was."

He stared down at her, looking back earnestly, and he knew he'd probably never get a better opening. "I feel the same way about meeting you."

She jerked backward, eyes wide, and dread overtook him. He'd pushed too much, too soon.

"Grant, you know…" She sighed, cutting herself off. "There's been something…more than friendship… between us all along."

"There has?" She'd felt it right away, too?

"Yes. But things have changed."

"Why?"

"You look at me differently now," she said softly, slipping out of his grasp and standing.

He got to his feet, too. "Maggie, that's just not true."

"I know you don't want it to be, but it is. I could feel it, before, when you kissed me."

Because of his mistake with her neck. He tried to argue, but she talked over him.

"That one day has affected *everything* in my life ever since. I joined the FBI because of it, I take a personal day every September 1 because of it, and every relationship I've ever had has tanked in one way or another because of it."

Her voice wavered, but there was certainty in her eyes as she said, "It's been ten years. I need to get to the other side of this. And I can't do it with you. Not with everything you know, with everything you've seen in my case file. I'm sorry," she finished quietly, then she turned and headed for the door.

Maggie squeezed her eyes shut and pressed a hand against the ache in her chest as she opened her car door.

From behind her, another hand reached out and slammed it shut.

As she whipped around, a woman out jogging paused and let out a cat call, then raced on past as Maggie realized Grant had followed her outside, in boxers, a T-shirt and bare feet.

She blinked, hoping Grant couldn't tell she was seconds from crying, and tried to turn her back on him. Just get in her car and drive home. Put this whole day behind her.

He took her arm and spun her around, something fierce in his expression as he told her, "The only thing that's different now is my feelings for you have gotten stronger, Maggie. If you're not interested, fine," he said, although his voice broke on the last word. "But if you're really worried I see you as somehow *less* because of what happened to you, that's just not true."

She pulled angrily out of his grip. "Look, Grant, maybe I've been giving you mixed signals, because I *am* interested. You know it. But it doesn't matter! What happened before—"

"When I almost touched your neck and I froze?" he asked bluntly.

"Yes." Some part of her actually wished he'd done it, that she'd had her inevitable panicked reaction. Maybe then she'd be able to admit to herself, once and for all, that it wasn't going to ever matter how the guy responded to learning about her past. That it was *her.* That she was never going to be cut out for a normal relationship.

She gulped and hung her head, not wanting him to see that fear in her eyes. Because if anyone might, it was Grant.

"I just didn't want to hurt you," he said softly.

"You saw me as damaged," she said, and preempted the response he was trying to give, adding, "Maybe I do, too."

"Maggie." He put his hand under her chin, forcing it up so she was looking at him. "I don't think that. You're one of the strongest people I know. And you must know that about yourself, or you'd never have had the confidence to go out for SWAT."

"That's different."

"It's no different—"

"Yes, it is. Romantically, men find out and they look at me as if I'm...tainted." She hated even saying the word, hated believing it was true. But decent men, men she'd been interested in enough to go out with, had suddenly changed when she told them. They'd begun looking at her as though she was a victim, and worse, as though she was somehow a different person than before. Unintentionally, she was sure, but to her—being on the other end of it—that didn't matter.

"Oh, Maggie," Grant sighed, and he sounded so sorry for her, she just wanted to leave.

She reached for her door handle again, but he drew her hands to his chest.

"The only person tainted by any of this was him. You came out of that stronger." His face was as serious as she'd ever seen it as he told her, "That's my theory on why he's threatening to come back for you, and not any of the others."

"I was first," Maggie said, feeling her shoulders slump with sudden exhaustion.

"Sort of," he said. "The first with the brand, anyway. But I don't think that's really why. I said from the start that it's because he couldn't break you. It's why his sick little obsession with you didn't end that day. You were too strong for him. You always will be."

She stared up at him, the anger and weariness fading underneath hope and fear that mingled together in equal measure.

He must have seen it, because he insisted, "What happened to you changes *nothing* about how I feel about you."

She blinked at him, her pulse beginning to race. "Prove it."

He went completely still for a few seconds that seemed to stretch out forever, then he peeled the keys out of her hand, hit the lock button and put his hands on her face, leaning in.

A car driving by honked, and Maggie jumped. "Not here."

"Okay." He bent down and with one smooth motion, picked her up and tossed her over his shoulder.

She was so surprised, she let out a burst of laughter, and suddenly the tension that always seemed to fill her broke apart. But nervousness quickly settled in its place.

They were back inside before she had a chance to figure out how to handle her anxiety. Then he was setting her down and bringing his hands back up to cup her cheeks, his thumbs caressing her skin before his lips slowly descended on hers.

Just like the other times he'd kissed her, she marveled at how soft and gentle his lips were. It was such a contrast to the hard muscles in his arms that she felt as she ran her fingers upward to tangle around his neck.

They stood there for a long time, his mouth pressing softly and sweetly against hers, his tongue teasing the seam of her lips, until she couldn't take it anymore, and she pushed up on her tiptoes and wound her leg around his.

Finally, he slid his hands down her back, pausing just long enough to unstrap her holster and set it on the mantel. Then his hands drifted lower, gripping her thighs. Pinpoints of pleasure danced over her skin where he touched her, and he lifted her up. As soon as she wrapped her legs around his waist and thrust her tongue into his mouth, he turned, heading straight for the couch.

Ripping her mouth from his, she panted, "Bedroom," then stared back at him, waiting, hoping he wouldn't stop the way he had the last time she'd made that request.

Instead, he smiled at her, one of those huge grins she'd always been drawn to, and strode down the hall as though he couldn't get there fast enough. He flipped on the light in his bedroom, and she had a brief impression of framed art on the wall, an open closet filled with suits on one side and cargos and T-shirts on the other, and a king-size bed.

She expected him to place her back on that bed, but

he turned around and sat on the edge, so she was sitting on top of him. He didn't give her time to decide if that was because he was afraid she wouldn't like someone over her; his hands slipped underneath her blouse and started stroking the curve of her waist. He ran his tongue along the outside of her ear, and need pulsed through her.

"Grant," she moaned, shocked at how desperate she sounded as she grabbed fistfuls of his shirt and tugged it over his head.

"Mmm," he responded, then turned back and fused his mouth to hers, simultaneously unbuttoning her blouse and sliding it off her arms.

As soon as it was off, she arched into him, loving the feel of his skin against hers. His hands started to head back to her waist, so she took hold of them and directed them to the button on her pants.

He undid them fast, then flipped her over onto her back, standing up and pulling the pants slowly down her legs, his gaze traveling the same path.

She propped herself up on her elbows to watch him there in nothing but his boxers, and when his eyes met hers, the pure desire she saw made her smile. In that instant, she was absolutely certain he wasn't thinking of anything in her past. Only her. Only right now.

She crooked her finger at him, and he smiled back at her, a smile full of anticipation and want and something else, something powerful that told her this was going to be more than a fling between friends. That maybe she'd found something much, much stronger.

Her breath caught as he lowered himself slowly on top of her, until she couldn't wait any longer. She had to wrap her arms and legs around him and arch up to meet his mouth.

Practically the instant his lips touched hers, a sudden ringing jolted her out of the moment.

He swore and glanced at the phone lit up on his nightstand, then down at her, then back again. Letting out a few more curses, he rolled over, bringing her with him so she was lying on top of him and making her laugh as he whispered, "Shhh," and picked up the phone.

"Work," he said, his voice suddenly serious and grim as he answered. "Grant Larkin."

Maggie could hear just enough to tell it was Kammy, but not enough to know what was happening. But there was no mistaking the all-business expression that wiped away the desire that had been on Grant's face seconds before. "Okay, I'm heading there now," he said, and hung up.

"What is it?" Maggie asked, propping herself up on her elbows so she could look down at him.

"The Hoffmeier family is taking a little impromptu vacation. There's a flight plan scheduled on their private jet leaving in less than an hour. I've got to go meet the plane." He pressed a fast kiss to her lips, then sat up, lifting her with him. "I've got to go."

Chapter Eleven

Grant was pissed off as he bullied his way onto the private airfield, using his Bureau credentials, his badge and his best SWAT scare tactics. What timing that the Hoffmeiers had to suddenly decide to leave DC. Really, really bad timing for him. And particularly suspicious timing for them.

"Heading to Florida, are you?" Grant called as he approached the midsize Cessna private jet being loaded with baggage as a man and woman stood beside it, looking impatient.

They both turned as he approached. The man was late sixties, with a shock of white hair and the kind of grimace on his face that looked as if it was permanently embedded there. Despite the warm August weather, he was wearing a lightweight suit. Beside him, the woman looked a few years younger, but she'd clearly tried to stave away the years with plastic surgery and dye. The result was too-plump lips, too-high eyebrows and unnaturally blond hair. She'd topped the look off with a candy-pink skirt suit, a floppy hat and oversize sunglasses.

"It's so lovely this time of year in Naples," Lorraine Hoffmeier replied, while her husband just scowled.

"I thought this was the rainy season," Grant said as he reached them and held out a hand. "Grant Larkin, FBI."

Lorraine took his hand limply, looking sideways at her husband, Frederik, who ignored it entirely.

"This is a private airstrip," he snapped.

"Not to me," Grant said, glancing over at the pair of men loading up the Hoffmeiers' luggage. It was going to take a while. "Long trip?"

"We're—" Lorraine started, but Frederik cut her off.

"If you have a business question, you can go through my office," Frederik said, peeling off a shiny business card and handing it over.

Grant pocketed it without a glance. "I don't. I have a family question."

Lorraine shuffled on tall heels that couldn't have been comfortable in the eighty-degree heat, and Frederik snapped, "I don't know what you think you're doing, harassing my family, son, but I know people over at the FBI. Whatever you're here for, it's not sanctioned, and your supervisor will be hearing about it."

Grant gave him a hard smile in return. "My supervisor is aware that I'm here. The Hoffmeier name has come up in connection with a case. I have a few simple questions for you, so that *I* don't have to kick this up to the next level."

Frederik turned to face Grant, leveling him with a look that had probably served him well in boardrooms for the past forty-five years. But this wasn't a boardroom, and Grant didn't intimidate easily.

"I know my rights. I don't have to answer a thing," Frederik said.

Grant shrugged, as though it didn't matter to him either way. "You don't. I can reach out to your employees, business associates and other family members next. Maybe they'll be more willing to cooperate in our investigation. Especially when they learn what we're investigating."

"I keep an attorney on retainer, son. I don't think you or the FBI wants a slander suit." His voice was hard and steady, but his jaw quivered.

Beside him, Lorraine had hunched down, and she'd crossed her arms over her chest.

"It's only slander if it's not true," Grant reminded him, then shrugged again and started to turn. "I'm surprised you don't even want to know what the investigation's about."

"What's it about?" Lorraine burst, like he'd gambled she would.

He turned slowly back around. "It's a serial rape case."

Lorraine turned so pale Grant thought he might have to catch her if she fell over, and Frederik sounded insulted when he said, "This is outrageous!"

"Obviously, you're not suspects," Grant said with the friendliest smile he could manage. "But your son has a connection to one of the victims, and we think he might be able to help us identify the person who did it."

Frederik's lips thinned into a straight line, but it was Lorraine who stiffened and said, "Jeffrey would not associate with a rapist. And I'm afraid he's unavailable. He's been living abroad for many years."

"Oh, I didn't say Jeffrey associated with him," Grant said, choosing his words carefully. "But he might have some key information to point us in the right direction."

Lorraine shook her head. "He's not here."

"That's okay. I just need some contact information." Grant took out a pen and notepad. "Phone number, address. I won't take much of his time."

Frederik and Lorraine stared at one another, seeming to have a silent communication, until Frederik gave one brief nod, and Lorraine pulled out her phone with shaking hands. "All I have is a cell phone number." She read a number off to him, which he jotted down.

"What about an address?"

Lorraine shook her head. "He moves around a lot. You know how some kids backpack across Europe?" She waved a still-shaky hand, encrusted with rings, in the air. "He never got over it."

"Where was he living the last time you talked to him?" Grant asked, trying to keep the annoyance out of his voice.

"I really don't know," Lorraine said, a long-simmering frustration in her tone. "He told me he was in Europe. That's all. I gave up trying to get more from Jeffrey a long time ago. The boy likes his privacy."

"Is he planning to come back to DC this summer?"

"Summer's about over, son," Frederik said, seeming to get his equilibrium back.

"I know. But September seems a perfect time to visit DC."

Lorraine's eyes narrowed, but confusion knitted her brow, as if she suspected there was more to his words, but she didn't know what. Beside her, her husband just frowned.

"You have the number," Frederik spoke up. "Now we need to get on our way." He turned toward the two men who'd almost finished loading the plane. "Let's get moving!"

The pilot who'd just come over from the closest building in time to overhear Frederik's demand, looked at them, then at his clipboard. He held out a hand to Frederik. "Just the three of you, sir?"

"Not him," Frederik said.

"I thought there were three passengers?" the pilot asked.

"Sorry I'm late!" someone called from behind him,

and before Grant turned around, he saw Lorraine smile widely and Frederik's scowl deepen.

The woman walking toward them in an expensive-looking skirt and blouse made Grant feel light-headed.

He must have been gaping because she tilted her head, gave him a perplexed look and asked, "Are you working security for my father?"

"Claudia Hoffmeier," he said. He'd known the Hoffmeiers had a daughter, younger than Jeffrey by six years, but he'd never seen a picture.

"That's right." She stood there, giving him an obvious appraisal.

He was probably staring right back, although his expression had to be a little more of the just-seen-a-ghost variety.

Claudia Hoffmeier had dark hair that hung halfway down her back, sky-blue eyes and a trim, athletic figure. Her gaze was direct, her stance assured, and her neck long and elegant, although he doubted hers sported a hook on the back. But she looked a lot like Maggie. A lot like eight other pictures stapled to case files.

He did the math in his head, realizing she was the same age as Maggie, too.

Various scenarios ran through his head, and he wasn't happy with any of them. It seemed pretty doubtful that Jeff Hoffmeier's name would come up in connection with a rape case, and his sister just *happened* to look like the victims. But what sort of deranged personality raped women who resembled his little sister? What would the motivation be? Some misplaced revenge for a sibling rivalry? An inappropriate attachment? Both?

"What?" she asked, sounding amused. "We know each other?"

"No," he said, his voice not quite right. "But I think there's someone in common we both know."

"Oh, yeah?" she asked, just as Frederik stepped forward and grabbed her arm. "Who's that?"

"Maggie Delacorte," he said, taking a chance and wishing he'd done more background on Claudia.

The smile instantly dropped off her face, and she stumbled, though he couldn't be sure if it was his question or her father yanking her away.

"Uh, sorry, no," she said, shaking her head. "I don't think so."

"Does Jeffrey know her?" he asked, getting louder and following as Frederik dragged Claudia toward the plane.

Lorraine moved more slowly, looking between them.

"I don't like this line of questioning, son," Frederik said, spinning and holding his hand up.

"Dad," Claudia said. "It's fine. Who are you, exactly?"

"Grant Larkin, FBI."

Her forehead furrowed as she studied him for a moment, and then she reached into a purse that probably cost more than he made in a month and handed him a card. "I have no idea if Jeffrey knows this woman, but I doubt it. He's lived abroad a long time. But whatever this is about, we're happy to help."

She tapped the card he was holding, and he finally glanced down at it. Claudia Hoffmeier, Attorney-at-Law, General Counsel for Hoffmeier Financial.

"Go ahead, Dad," she said, ushering him toward the jet, then looking back at Grant. "You have questions, feel free to give me a call, Mr. Larkin."

Then she and her parents boarded the plane, and Grant moved back, heading numbly toward his own vehicle, still staring at the card and pondering Claudia Hoffmeier's reaction.

Did she recognize Maggie's name? Did her parents know their son had done something they should be worried about? *Was* Jeffrey really living abroad?

Putting the card away, Grant doubled his speed. He needed to go to the office, call the number Lorraine had provided for Jeffrey and see if he could get a lead on where it pinged to, and check out the entire Hoffmeier family.

GRANT CURSED AS he hung up his cell phone, wishing he was using a landline he could slam down, maybe a few times. "Out of service," he told Kammy.

She looked unsurprised as she nodded at him from across the conference table at the WFO.

He'd called her back there after visiting the Hoffmeiers, and he could tell she'd been planning to make it an early night, just like him. She'd swapped the suit she seemed to own in every shade of black, blue and gray for linen pants and a T-shirt, and scrubbed her face clean of makeup. It should have made her seem more approachable, but somehow she still looked every bit the hard-driving FBI supervisor.

"You think Lorraine Hoffmeier gave you a dead number on purpose?" Kammy asked.

"I don't know. When I asked about Jeff coming back to visit in September, she gave me this look that said she knew I was alluding to something, but she didn't know what. The father and sister, on the other hand…"

"You think they're knowingly covering up for a serial rapist? That would make them accessories. If she's a lawyer—"

"I think they suspect. And I think they're trying to distance themselves from him, protect their family name.

It's why I was hoping they'd cooperate, so if it *does* turn out to be him, they'll look like they have clean hands."

Kammy braced her elbows on the table and leaned forward. "Let me ask you a question, Grant. Something here stinks, that's for sure, but we've only really connected Jeff Hoffmeier to Shana Mills. What if she's the only victim? Maybe the family found out and suggested he take to backpacking in Europe."

Grant swallowed his instant reaction, which was to argue, and thought about it. "Well, assuming we're talking first-degree sexual assault, statute of limitations in DC generally runs out after fifteen years. But he didn't leave right after Shana's attack. He left DC ten years ago, after Maggie's."

"Maybe the family found out later?"

"It's possible, but that's some coincidental timing."

"Unless he really is in Europe. In which case, he's not a possibility at all. If he's here, he's stayed way below the radar. You think the family's supplying him with wads of cash? He'd have to stick to places that weren't running credit checks. That means no house rentals, nothing. You think a kid with his background is living that low to ground?"

"Or the family money supplied him with forged documents," Grant suggested, then he did pound his fist on the table. "I should have pushed harder, not let them get on that plane."

"We had no reason to compel them to stay," Kammy reminded him. "And the sister is a lawyer, so she knew that, even if the parents didn't."

"Oh, Frederik Hoffmeier knew. That's the other thing. He handed me a business card, tried to kick me off the airfield as soon as I showed up. Had no interest in even hearing what case I was investigating."

"He owns a big, successful business," Kammy said. "I'm not sure that's a smoking gun. This guy has been investigated before."

"Yeah, I know," Grant said. "Securities fraud. It might not have stuck, but you'd think going through an investigation again would worry him. You'd think he'd want to at least *pretend* to cooperate. Besides, even after I told him it was family-related, he didn't want to talk to me."

"Again, that's not a cry of guilt. You're suggesting that this man knows—or at least suspects—his son has abducted, raped and branded nine women in the past decade. That's some pretty strong family loyalty."

"I've seen it before," Grant said. "I'm sure you have, too."

She sighed and nodded. "Yeah. But for something this serious and long-running? I'd say he'd be the exception. And what about the sister? An intelligent, high-powered lawyer who's willing to keep her brother's sick secret? Especially when it involves him attacking other women, ones who look like her?"

"A high-powered lawyer who works for the family business," Grant reminded her. "A thirty-two-year-old woman who reacted when I said Maggie's name."

"Who reacted when you said my name?"

Grant looked toward the door of the conference room as Maggie strode in, wearing the gray dress pants and short-sleeved blouse she'd shown up in at his house. But his mind instantly flashed to how he'd seen her last: stretched out in his bed in nothing but a dark blue bra and panties. Her hair haloed out behind her on the bed, her lips swollen from kissing him.

Maggie flushed, and he realized his thoughts must have been showing, so he quickly looked away, before Kammy saw, too.

Kammy glanced back at him suspiciously, but Grant fiddled with the file in front of him until he was sure he had control of his emotions, then he looked up, all business, and told Maggie, "Claudia Hoffmeier."

The very next call he'd made after talking to Kammy on his drive over to WFO had been to Maggie. She'd still been waiting at his house, and he'd fought the instinct to call Kammy off and just go home to Maggie. The idea was so appealing, even the thought of her waiting in his house made his body heat up.

But the case was too important, and he was onto something with Jeff Hoffmeier. He was sure of it.

Maggie frowned as she walked around the long table and sat down next to him. "The name doesn't sound familiar."

Grant reached for Kammy's open laptop and turned it toward Maggie. "This is her." The picture was from the Hoffmeier corporate website, and for the millionth time that night, Grant wished he'd looked it up on his phone on the drive over to the airport.

Maggie studied Claudia's photo, either not noticing or not commenting on the similarities between them. Finally, she shook her head. "I don't recognize her. What's the connection?"

"She's your age. And look at her bio. She went to your college at the same time you were there."

"So did thousands of other students. She said she knew me?"

"She claimed she *didn't* know you. But she definitely reacted when I said your name. And it hasn't been in the papers, so there's no reason for her to recognize it."

"And you think, what?" Maggie asked. "That she knows her brother is the Fishhook Rapist?"

"I think she suspects," Grant said, just as Kammy mused, "The Fishhook Rapist."

"What?" Grant glanced over at her.

Kammy dug through the file in front of her, then set the picture of Jeffrey Hoffmeier on the table. "How does a rich kid get a name like that?"

Maggie paled a little, but she said, "You mean why the brand of a hook?"

"Exactly," Kammy said, clearly uncomfortable as she stared back at Maggie. "What connection does he have to the fishing industry?"

"Maybe it's random," Maggie suggested. "Something to throw investigators off track?"

"No," Kammy said adamantly. "The profiler we had look at this a few years back said this hook is his signature. You know what that means, right?"

"It's the thing he's compelled to do. It matters to him," Maggie replied, her tone professional, as though it wasn't her own case they were discussing. "So it must mean something. There has to be a connection. You're right." She looked questioningly at Grant.

He frowned. "We can search for a connection, but I think we should put our resources into finding this guy. Let's talk to Interpol."

"We need more than your gut to get Interpol involved," Kammy said.

"Okay, fine. I don't think he's in Europe, anyway. I think he's here."

"And what if you're wrong?"

The question came from Kammy, but Grant looked at Maggie. If this were any other case, he'd push to follow his instincts, but it wasn't any other case. For him, this one was all about Maggie. And he'd never be able to forgive himself if they let the Fishhook Rapist slip through their fingers because they were following his stubborn lead on the wrong guy.

"What if I tried calling Claudia?" Maggie suggested.

"She's on a flight to Florida," Grant reminded her.

"Yeah, but it's a private plane. She could have her cell phone on."

"What are you hoping to gain from that?" Kammy asked.

"Shock value. See if we can figure out how she knows me."

"She's a lawyer," Kammy reminded her. "I don't think—"

"A lawyer," Maggie repeated, looking pensive.

"What is it?" Grant asked.

"See if you can find a picture of her from college."

"I'll try," Grant said, dragging the laptop toward him again and starting a search.

"I took a prelaw class right before my senior year. There was a girl in my class—I can't remember her name—but we did a project together. We weren't friends or anything, so I don't remember a lot about her, but I do recall we did well on that project. She suggested I could intern at her family's company—that I should apply once I finished my undergrad degree. It was so long ago, and after…what happened…I decided not to go to law school, anyway, so I totally forgot about it."

Maggie had once planned to go to law school? Grant glanced sideways at her, surprised. He knew her decision to join the FBI had come because of her assault, but he couldn't imagine her doing anything else. She was such a natural on the SWAT missions, and he assumed she ran case investigations with the same intense, focused tenacity.

"You think this girl was Claudia?" Kammy asked. "Did you ever meet her brother?"

"It's possible it was Claudia." Maggie shook her head. "I just don't remember. It was only a weeklong project. And it was ten years ago. It was the very end of the summer semester and I didn't end up taking more prelaw classes my senior year, so she fell off my radar. But as for meeting her brother? If I did, it wasn't through her. We never talked outside of class. I was surprised when she mentioned the internship thing."

"So you never interviewed for it?" Kammy pushed.

"No."

"I've got her," Grant said, turning the computer so Maggie could see the grainy yearbook image. It was amazing what you could find on the internet.

He pointed to the girl at the end of the dorm picture. "That's Claudia, from ten years ago."

Maggie squinted at it, her teeth catching her bottom lip, and Grant forced himself to stop staring before Kammy suspected there was something between them—if she didn't already.

"Is that her?" Kammy pushed.

"It could be," Maggie said slowly, not sounding certain. "This picture looks sort of familiar."

"What about the company? Hoffmeier Financial?" Grant asked.

"Hoffmeier Financial? That's what their family business is called?" Maggie's eyes drifted upward, and he could tell she was trying to remember. "You know, it might be her, then. I remember the company didn't sound like a typical law firm, so I asked about it, and she said it wasn't a law firm at all. But she said they had a lawyer on staff, and that she had the position lined up as soon as she graduated."

Grant nodded at Kammy. "Claudia has been working for her father's company since she graduated from law school."

"What about Jeff?" Kammy asked. "They promised Claudia their general counsel position, but nothing for him?"

"Well, he obviously hasn't worked there in the past decade," Grant answered. "Before that, I don't know. He would have been twenty-eight a decade ago, so it's possible he worked for the company before he left for Europe, assuming that's what hc did."

"And if he didn't actually go to Europe, maybe he quit when he dropped off the map a decade ago." Kammy nodded. "It's worth checking out."

"When exactly did he disappear?" Maggie asked, her hands clutched too tightly in her lap.

"December is the last time his name shows up on ownership documents," Grant said, "So a few months afterward."

"What did he own?" Kammy asked. "A house?"

"An apartment."

"Not a likely spot to bring his victims, then," she concluded.

"What about the parents' house?" Grant suggested.

"That would be risky," Kammy said. "But worth looking into, I suppose. Maybe they were away. Let's dig deeper on Jeff and see what we can find."

"Thanks for coming back in," Maggie said softly.

"Whoever it is, we're catching him. And if it is Jeff, and his family knew, I don't care how connected they are. We'll make sure they pay for it, too."

Grant nodded at Kammy, pleased by the intensity in her voice. "Let's get to it." He tried to sound confident, but he'd already spent time hunting for Jeff and hadn't come up with any solid leads.

Praying tonight they'd find the break they needed, he told them, "I'll check into his connection to the company."

An hour later, he stared at what he'd found, surprised. "Jeff *did* work for Hoffmeier Financial. He went to college out of state—where he apparently spent most of his time partying—and then moved back and started working for his dad. I've got some buried arrests from that time period, and from when he was at school. Apparently Dad kept having to bail him out of trouble."

"What kind of arrests?" Maggie asked.

"A couple of DUIs, some resisting arrest and assaulting a police officer charges related to cops breaking up a party at his college fraternity house back in Palo Alto when he was still a student. Plus a handful of other charges, mostly minor stuff, but a few assault charges that got pushed under the rug once he moved back to DC after he graduated. Not sexual," he clarified. "Mostly seems to be him getting into bar fights."

"So what happened? Why did he leave the family business?" Kammy asked.

"It seems that Frederik Hoffmeier got sick of his son's work ethic and kicked him out of the company."

"What was his position while he was there?" Maggie wondered.

"Vice President," Grant replied. At her raised eyebrows, he added, "Hoffmeier Financial had three back then, and from what I can tell, Jeff's was mostly in name only."

"So he got kicked out of the family business and left DC," Kammy summed up.

"No," Grant said, "He got kicked out of the family

business, and hung out in DC for another year, dating college girls and blowing through his trust fund."

"What's that?" Maggie said just as he was about to tell them more about Jeff's wastrel lifestyle.

"What?" Grant asked, glancing at her.

Her whole face had tightened as she leaned toward his computer.

"I found an old archived image of the Hoffmeier website, listing executives."

"In the corner," Maggie said, her voice as tense as her expression.

Grant leaned closer, too. "The logo. That's weird," he realized. "It looks like the current logo was cut in half from this original one." He clicked to enlarge it and then felt his jaw drop.

"It's him," Maggie choked out.

"How do you know?" Kammy asked, standing up and moving behind them to see the screen.

Grant pointed. The current Hoffmeier Financial logo resembled the top half of a family crest, but the original logo had been the entire thing. And the bottom half of the crest contained three distinct fishing hooks.

Chapter Twelve

Maggie glanced around her at the near-empty WFO office and then opened the picture of Jeff Hoffmeier on her computer screen. Except for the initial reaction she'd had to him, she still didn't recognize him.

Yet for her, the hooks on the family crest—and Hoffmeier Financial's sudden logo change about a decade ago—cinched it. Jeff had to be the Fishhook Rapist.

Kammy and Grant were theorizing that he might have actually used something with the family crest on it to make the brand. On her own, Maggie had told Ella about it, and she agreed, saying it was a good bet Jeff had used the crest because he harbored hatred toward his family for cutting him out of the business.

From an investigative perspective, the fishhooks had led them off track, because the FBI had long theorized the rapist was in the fishing industry. The reality was that the Hoffmeier family *had* been in fishing—but centuries ago, back in Germany.

From a psychological perspective, Ella had told Maggie that Jeff had probably used the hook as a way to try to implicate his family. Not that he was trying to get himself—or them—caught, but that he got a sick thrill out of branding something so intimately connected to the family that had rejected him onto the women he was trying to mark with a type of ownership.

Ella had also been the one to point out that Jeff's firing from the company business had happened only two years after Shana Mills's attack. He'd gotten away with that assault, giving him the confidence that he could do it again, and a plan had started to form in his mind. At least that was Ella's theory.

She'd continued to profile that he probably particularly resented his brunette, blue-eyed sister, for getting the place he thought he deserved as the firstborn son. That, too, would have happened within a year of Jeff's being pushed out.

So Maggie already fit his "type." She looked like both Shana Mills and Claudia Hoffmeier—the two women he simultaneously loved and hated, in different ways. And the rest of the known Fishhook Rapist victims fit, too. But Ella thought Jeff might have targeted her specifically because he learned his sister had offered her a job at the company that wanted nothing to do with him.

It made her sick just thinking about it, especially if Claudia knew—or suspected—what he'd done to her afterward, and said nothing. And there was a good chance she had, since the Hoffmeiers had cut the family crest in half, using only the top part for their company logo, after he'd begun his attacks.

Grant and Kammy had been back to talk to Shana Mills, to see if she had any idea where Jeff might be, and to get more insight into that relationship. Grant had returned from the visit convinced that Shana had been his first rape victim, and that he'd gotten power out of the fact that drugging her prevented her from realizing it was him. He hadn't told Maggie that; she'd overheard it.

It had instantly made her think about what else she

knew about Shana and Jeff's relationship: that they'd dated again after Shana's rape. Maggie's whole body chilled at the idea that Shana hadn't realized she was going out with the same man who'd hurt her.

It was bad enough that Jeffrey Hoffmeier was a rapist, but what kind of sociopath dated the woman he'd assaulted, secretly feeling empowered because she didn't know? The answer was the kind of sociopath she wanted behind bars for the rest of his sorry life.

But when she'd pushed to find out everything else Grant and Kammy knew, she'd learned that with only three days left until September 1, it wasn't enough. It wasn't anywhere near enough.

Staring at Jeff's picture all the time wasn't telling her anything new, either. Because just like Shana, she didn't remember the person who'd hurt her. And it wasn't doing her any good obsessively staring at him, hoping a memory would surface. The reality was that even if one did, it probably wouldn't help them find him now.

Closing the image, Maggie shut down her computer and headed for the conference room. It had become her last stop of the day. Sometimes the whole team working the case was there, but often Maggie stayed late, waiting until everyone had gone home except Kammy and Grant, who were working later and later each night as the deadline drew closer.

Her own supervisor had already approached her and told her that in two days, if they didn't have Jeff under arrest, they were putting her in protective custody. Even though she was officially off the team, she still felt like a SWAT agent, and she hated the idea of needing protection. But she wasn't about to turn it down.

Before she reached the conference room, Maggie's phone rang. Halting midstride, she checked the readout, then turned the other way, down the hall where the coffeepot was situated, for a little privacy from the few remaining agents in the bullpen. It was the investigator from OPR.

"Hello," she answered, hearing her nerves come through in the single word.

"Agent Delacorte, this is John from OPR. I'm sorry to call you in the evening."

"That's okay. I'm still at the office," she said, trying to calm her voice. OPR calling her meant they'd made a decision about the incident that had caused her to leave SWAT.

"I wanted you to know that we came to a decision. The incident will go in your personnel file," he began, but she'd expected that.

It was the least of her worries.

When she didn't say anything, just waited, her breath stalled, he continued, "Your teammates think very highly of you. Every one of them spoke up on your behalf."

Her eyes got watery at the idea that all the guys still wanted to work with her, that they still trusted her in a firefight after she'd frozen at such a critical moment. That included Grant, even though he was the one who'd paid for her error, but she realized that part didn't surprise her. Grant always stood by her.

The thought stuck with her even as John continued, "Until the investigation into the Fishhook Rapist is concluded, you're to stay on only your civil rights squad duties. However, after that time, you're free to rejoin SWAT."

They'd cleared her.

Maggie gasped, then stuttered, "Th-thank you."

"Don't thank me," John said. "Thank your teammates. They were very convincing that you're an asset to SWAT.

Between them and your excellent record there over the past four years, we agree."

Relief washed over Maggie stronger than she'd expected as John hung up, and she doubled over with the knowledge that she hadn't let the Fishhook case destroy her SWAT career.

It didn't mean she'd be going back, though. When the Fishhook case was over, there was going to be another stumbling block: Grant.

She had no idea how to define their relationship, but there was no question they had one that went beyond the scope of teammates. She wasn't willing to give up whatever was developing between them, which meant one of them would have to leave SWAT.

Maybe a spot would eventually open up on another team, but it was rare. And it wouldn't be the same. Her SWAT team had become like family.

The very idea of leaving left a knot in her chest, but Maggie straightened, vowing to worry about it later. Right now, she needed to find out the status of the case.

She hurried through the bullpen, past the only two agents still cloistered in their cubicles, and into the conference room. The room was an organized mess. The files and documents covering every surface seemed to have tripled in the past week as they tried to hunt down Jeff Hoffmeier.

Grant and Kammy sat in their usual seats at the far end of the room, and both looked up at her with bloodshot eyes as she entered.

"What happened?" Grant asked, standing.

"Nothing. I just heard back from OPR."

"I'll give you a minute," Kammy said, getting tiredly to her feet. When Maggie started to protest, she added, "I need caffeine, anyway, or I'll be down for the count."

She headed out the door, closing it behind her, and Grant was instantly at Maggie's side. "How did it go?"

"They told me you spoke for me."

"Of course."

"You're not worried—"

"What?" Grant cut her off. "That you'll have another flashback to a memory you didn't even know you had, when responding to a SWAT call? What are the chances of that? Probably as slim as my MP-5 misfiring."

"That could happen," Maggie said.

"Exactly. Or Clive could have a heart attack on a call. But the chances are much higher that none of those things will happen, so why lose one of the best members of the team?"

"You think I'm one of the best members on the team?"

"And the cutest," he teased, then got serious. "I do, but it was Clive who told OPR that part."

Wow. Her team leader thought she was one of his best agents? That was high praise from Clive. "Well, it's official, but I'm not sure what I'll do. You know, with everything between us…"

She stopped as Kammy came back in the room, practically gulping from a coffee mug.

"We'll figure it out," Grant said, pressing his hand against her upper arm before he returned to his seat.

Maggie followed more slowly, more torn than ever. She'd felt vindicated to hear she was still on the team, then conflicted because of Grant, and now even more conflicted hearing how her teammates viewed her. She couldn't deny whatever was happening with her and Grant. If they were going to be serious, one of them had to leave the team. She'd been there for four years, so it seemed only fair that it be his turn on SWAT now. But how could she leave the team after their vote of support?

Pushing the worry to the back of her mind, Maggie focused on the more immediate problem. "Do you have anything new?"

"A new reason September 1 is Jeffrey Hoffmeier's date of choice," Kammy said.

"What do you mean?"

Kammy gestured to Grant, and he said, "I kept digging for old information about Jeffrey from eleven years ago, when his family pushed him out of the company, and I found a press release. It announced that Jeffrey was leaving the company as VP and named some other guy who was taking his place. It was dated September 1."

She felt a wave of hot anger, "So he's using part of the crest to punish them, and that—plus Shana Mills's attack is why he picked September 1? Because it's a date that ties to both Shana and Claudia and his family?"

"Looks like it," Grant said.

"Have you been able to track him?"

"Well, we've confirmed that he had a pretty sizable trust fund, although what happened to it all is questionable," Kammy said. "We think at least some of the money went into foreign banks and was hidden under shell companies. We've got some of our White Collar agents digging around, but they're not likely to be able to untangle that mess in the next three days."

"Claudia Hoffmeier isn't answering at the number she gave us, and neither are her parents," Grant said, clearly frustrated. "And we're trying to get some warrants to get the family property information—whatever we can't dig up on our own—but it's not happening."

Maggie nodded, angry but unsurprised. She was sure it was Jeff Hoffmeier now, but what did they have, evidence-wise, really? A lot of conjecture, some suspicious timing and a family crest with an element that, while it wasn't typical, definitely wasn't unique to the Hoffmeiers.

"What about the property we do know about?" Maggie asked. "He must be in DC at this point."

How close had he gotten to her? Maggie shuddered, thankful Grant was looking at Kammy and didn't notice.

Kammy set her empty coffee mug down, seeming significantly more awake. "The Hoffmeiers have a house in the city, and another in horse country in Virginia. Claudia has one here and an apartment in Maryland, where her boyfriend lives. Beyond that, we don't know, but we've already found a couple of shell companies with Frederik's name on them, so we're digging deeper there."

"But even if you find something, you can't get on the property," Maggie summed up.

Grant glanced at her, and the expression on his face told her that if the deadline hit and they hadn't caught the guy, procedure was going right out the window.

She started to shake her head at him, then realized there was no way he'd be kicking down doors on September 1, because he'd be wherever *she* was, standing beside her. Or, really, knowing Grant, he'd be standing in front of her, wearing Kevlar and holding a Glock.

A smile quivered on her lips, and he looked back at her questioningly, but she didn't get a chance to say anything, because her phone rang again.

She glanced at the readout and rolled her eyes. "Scott," she told them. "I'm running late. He probably expected me at the house two minutes ago and is panicking."

She stood and hurried out of the conference room to answer, not wanting to distract them any more than she already was by constantly seeking out updates. "Hey, Scott, I'll be leaving the office in a few minutes, I promise. I just—"

"Don't leave," Scott said, panic in his voice that made fear creep along her nerve endings.

"What's wrong?"

"I'm not at your house," Scott said, and it was so obvious he was trying not to worry her that it was making it worse.

"Why not? What happened?"

"There was a break-in at my house," Scott said, and his voice got choked up as he finished, "Chelsie was shot."

Shock made her go rigid, then pain seemed to explode in her chest. Her voice came out too high when she asked, "Is she okay?"

"I'm driving to the hospital right now. I'll call you with an update. All I know so far is that she's in surgery."

Maggie ran over to her cubicle and grabbed her purse. "I'm on my way to meet you."

"No," Scott replied. "Call Ella. Ask her to come over tonight and stay with you, okay?"

"Scott, I want to—"

"I can't stay with you every second at the hospital, Maggie. And that place is busy. I don't want someone coming in with a weapon and walking you out of there—"

"It's not September 1," Maggie reminded him. "That date *matters* to him. A lot. How would he even know about Chelsie, anyway?" Her legs wobbled and she sank onto her chair. "Did—"

"It's not him. They got a description from my neighbor, who happened to be out running at the time." Scott lived quite a distance from his closest neighbor, out in the country in Virginia. "The person who broke in was black. Not this Hoffmeier guy."

"Is it connected to what happened a few months ago?" Maggie asked. Chelsie had been targeted by some men with major resources, and Scott had been shot in that house protecting her. But she'd thought that nightmare was over.

"No. Local police called me, and they're pretty sure they know who it is. It looks like he was after money. He's a known druggie, and this isn't his first offense of this type."

"So let me come—"

"No," Scott said, his tone harsh and final. Then he said more calmly, "Please don't make me worry about you, too. I know my hospital scenario is me being overly paranoid, but humor me. Just call Ella. Promise me you won't go anywhere until you hear from her, and I'll let you know when Chelsie's out of surgery."

She heard Scott's tires squeal and then his car door slam and realized he must have arrived at the hospital.

"Okay," she promised. "Please call me when you know anything."

"I will," Scott said and hung up.

Maggie's hands shook as she did the same, then immediately dialed Ella. It went straight to voice mail, so she left a message telling Ella to call her, then walked slowly back to the conference room.

Grant lurched to his feet. "What happened?"

"There was a break-in at my brother's house. Chelsie was shot."

"Is she okay?" Grant reached for the holster he'd set on the cabinet behind him. "You need me to drive you to the hospital?"

Beside him, sympathy and frustration warred on Kammy's face.

"She's in surgery," Maggie said, walking to the end of the table and taking a seat. "Scott's going to call me when he knows anything. But I'm going to stay here until I hear from Ella."

"Good idea." Grant, who knew about Scott's and Ella's

determination not to let her out of their sight unless she was with other FBI agents, nodded approvingly. Then, ignoring Kammy, he slung an arm around her shoulders and gave her a hug. "Chelsie's almost as stubborn and strong as you are. She'll be okay."

"I hope so," Maggie said, then straightened, determined to distract herself. "I don't suppose anything new came up while I was on the call?"

"Actually," Grant surprised her, "I was running down a hunch, and I did find something."

"It's good," Kammy said, leaning toward them. "This might be enough to get us a warrant on the properties, if we follow the trail far enough."

"Or maybe some new places to look," Grant suggested.

Maggie's heart rate spiked. "What is it?"

"Since we weren't having any luck with Jeff's name showing up in any of the cities where the attacks occurred, I started checking into other family members." He leaned back in his seat, looking proud. "I got a hit. Another name that showed up in every city, at all the right times."

Shock pulsed through her. Had they been wrong? Had she been unable to recognize Jeff Hoffmeier because it wasn't actually him? Had her reaction to his picture been because he resembled the actual perpetrator, some other member of his family?

"Who is it?" Maggie choked out.

"Jeff's cousin. Different last name, which is why Hoffmeier didn't come up for us."

"What's his name?" Maggie asked. "Do you have a picture?"

"Yeah." Grant typed away on his computer, then turned it around.

A picture labeled Jasper Grimes filled the screen, and

he looked a lot like Jeff Hoffmeier. Slightly more angular features, bigger nose, not quite the same bright blue eyes. But close enough that it would explain her reaction to Jeff. Except…

She looked over at Grant. "I don't recognize him."

"No." Grant shook his head. "It's not him. Sorry, I should have been more clear. Jasper Grimes was in a car accident eleven years ago. He was badly injured. He made it through, but with severe brain trauma. He'd been living in a medical facility in Maryland ever since. It's not him using that ID."

"It's Jeff," Maggie realized. "He hasn't been in Europe. He's just been using his cousin's ID to stay under the radar."

"Exactly," Grant said. "Credit checks were fine, because Jasper's still alive—his ID is still good. And Jeff looks similar enough. So that's why we see Jeff popping up randomly in the states every few years. He uses his own ID to access his trust fund in some in-between state where there's no connection to the Fishhook cases, then keeps traveling and goes back to Jasper's ID."

"So," Maggie asked the most important question, "does Jasper Grimes own property in DC?"

"Let's find out," Grant said.

He and Kammy started searching, while Maggie tried not to think about how Chelsie was doing.

Finally, Grant sighed and glanced over at Kammy, who shook her head.

"Either he's not using Jasper's name here, or he's buried it under one of his dad's shell corporations. I can't find him."

Maggie tried not to feel discouraged. The information could still lead them to him. She had to think positive.

But all she could think of was the anniversary looming

over her. Three days from now, she wouldn't be gathered with Scott and Ella, praying no other victim would show up in the news reports.

She'd be surrounded by federal agents, in some undisclosed location, under protective custody.

If Jeff Hoffmeier couldn't find her, who would he go after instead? And how would she ever forgive herself when she heard that name?

Chapter Thirteen

"Come home with me."

Grant's request was met with silence from Maggie, as she stared up at him, seeming to only half comprehend.

They were still at the WFO, an hour after Kammy had gone home. An hour after the rest of the office had completely emptied out. Grant had promised himself he'd wait until she heard back from Scott about Chelsie before suggesting it, but it wasn't doing either of them any good being at the WFO.

The office was dark except for the conference room, which looked as though a tornado had hit it, dropping Fishhook Rapist detritus everywhere in its wake. Not exactly what Maggie needed to be surrounded by while she waited to hear the status of her friend's condition.

And although Grant was still searching for leads on the Jasper Grimes ID, he was heading rapidly for a wall of exhaustion, and he knew it.

"What about—" Maggie started, but jumped when her phone rang. She grabbed it, stress in her voice as she answered. "Scott? How is she?"

Grant tapped her arm, and Maggie hit speaker.

"She made it out of surgery." Scott's weary voice came over the speaker sounding tinny and far away.

"Thank goodness," Maggie said.

"There were no complications. The bullet went straight through, so she lost a lot of blood, but it didn't nick anything vital on its way. She got lucky."

As lucky as anyone who got shot could be, Grant thought, taking Maggie's hand in his.

She gave him a shaky smile, her eyes watery, then looked back at the phone. "She's going to be okay?"

"Yeah," Scott said. "But I'm staying with her here overnight. Not exactly protocol, but the FBI credentials are good for something."

"Good," Maggie said. "Did they catch the guy who did it?"

"Not yet." Scott's voice was instantly hard and angry. "But the police chief stopped by the hospital personally, and he tells me they're running down all of this guy's haunts. He's supposed to call me as soon as they have him in custody."

"Okay," Maggie said. "Let me know. And tell Chelsie I'm thinking about her, when she wakes up."

"I will," Scott said. "Am I on speaker? Is Ella there?"

"Uh, no," Maggie said. "I'm still at WFO. I called the BAU office and was told Ella's in a late meeting, so I'm waiting until she gets out to go anywhere."

"Do you need me to—" Scott started.

"No," Grant said. "I'm here with Maggie. If we don't hear from Ella soon, Maggie can come back to my house. I won't leave her alone."

"Thanks, man," Scott said, relief obvious in his voice. "Call me if you need anything."

"Don't worry," Maggie said, squeezing Grant's hand. "Just focus on Chelsie."

She hung up the phone and turned toward him. "Let me try Ella one more time."

He nodded at her, taking in the tension of her jaw, the

deep shadows under her eyes that hadn't been there six months ago. He stroked his fingers over hers, silently praying that they'd catch Hoffmeier and end this all for good.

He missed the light that used to come into her eyes when they did SWAT training, the easy way she'd joke with them at O'Reilley's after a call. He hated watching this weigh on her, and ten years was far too long.

Worry filled him, the fear that even having identified Hoffmeier, they wouldn't be able to catch the guy. He realized after a moment that he'd squeezed Maggie's hand even tighter.

She looked questioningly at him, and he lifted her hand to his lips, pressing a kiss on her knuckles that made a smile lift her face and a little of that light he loved come into her eyes.

"Go ahead and call Ella," he said, instead of telling her what was on his mind. "See if her meeting is over."

She dialed, then shook her head a minute later, looking frustrated as she set her phone down. "She's still not picking up." Nerves strained her voice when she said, "Do you think something's wrong?"

"I think her meeting is going late. Or maybe the profiler you called forgot to give her the message. She thought Scott was with you, right? She was planning to just go home. Maybe she's there, and she's got her phone in the other room or something, and can't hear it."

"Yeah, but maybe I should call Logan. Just to make sure." She checked her watch, then looked at Grant. "He's at work now. I didn't realize it was so late. You're probably exhausted."

He was, but that didn't matter. "I'm fine. Come on." He stood, pulling her up with him. "You can just as easily call Ella again from my house."

He'd expected her to drop his hand, but instead, she turned it and threaded her fingers through his as she tucked her phone in her pocket. "Okay. Getting out of here—" she gestured around her at the case information "—sounds really good."

"Let's go," he said, heading for the conference room door, their linked hands swinging between them making him ridiculously happy even with everything that was happening.

They'd almost reached the parking garage when Maggie's cell phone rang. She whipped it out of her pocket. "Ella," she said, pressing the phone to her ear.

Then she ground to a sudden halt. Her face went unnaturally pale as a stream of what sounded like gibberish to Grant burst from her phone.

"What is it?" he asked, wrapping an arm around her shoulders in case she was going to fall.

She held up her hand, listening to whatever Ella was telling her, as foreboding traveled up Grant's spine, raising goose bumps along the way.

"No, no," she finally spoke into the phone. "Scott's at the hospital with Chelsie. Break-in at their house. Chelsie's okay." There was a pause, then she sobbed, "I'm so sorry."

He watched her trying to get it together as Ella said something else, then Maggie assured her, "I'm with Grant at WFO. I won't leave his side. We've got three days. We know September 1 is too important to him, and the FBI is putting me in protective custody the day before. Go. Check on Logan. Call me when you know."

"What happened?" Grant asked as soon as she hung up.

Maggie's voice was barely above a whisper as she told him, "Ella is on her way to the hospital. Logan and his partner were called to the scene of a crime, where they were ambushed. Logan was hit." A sob escaped as she said, "They don't know if he's going to make it."

"This isn't random," Grant realized.

"It's my fault," she sobbed, and before Grant could argue, she finished, "It's the Fishhook Rapist, trying to take away the people who've always been beside me, so I'll be isolated. So I'll be all alone when he comes back for me in three…" She glanced at her phone, and he saw that it had just hit midnight. "Make that two days."

Chapter Fourteen

Maggie crossed her hands over her chest, a stubborn tilt to her chin Grant recognized from SWAT calls. "I'm not putting you in danger, too."

"Well, I'm not leaving you alone," Grant said, "and you know it. Would you feel better if I called the rest of the team? We can all camp out at my house. Or we can get the FBI to start the protective custody now."

"No," she responded instantly, standing her ground at the dark entrance to the WFO parking garage, where she'd halted as soon as she realized what Ella's call meant. "I'm not going into hiding, not with Logan and Chelsie in the hospital. Scott or Ella might need me."

"There's nothing you can do for them right now," Grant said, but he knew that trying to make her go anywhere while her brother and best friend were in trouble wasn't going to happen. Especially not when she was this angry.

At least she was furious and not terrified. Or at least, that's what she was letting him see.

"I've got two days until he comes for me," Maggie reminded him.

"I'm not sure we can count on that," Grant said. "Maybe he anticipated the FBI putting a detail on you, and he's trying to strike early. Why would he go after

Logan and Chelsie today if he wasn't coming after you for another two days?"

"They were both shot," Maggie burst out. "They'll be in the hospital at least that long. And it's the psychology of it. He's been playing mind games with me for months, with those sick letters. This is more of it. He's drawing everyone I love away from me, and I'm not letting you put yourself in harm's way, too."

"You don't have a choice," Grant said softly, folding her hand into his. Her slim, pale fingers looked so small and delicate next to his bigger, darker hand.

"Ella and Scott have been beside you for ten years. They're long-term staples in your life he would obviously anticipate. But Hoffmeier doesn't know about me. And look, I think we should assume the worst, but honestly, I agree with you about the date. We know September 1 is symbolic to him. I'm not sure why he went after your friends early, but I think he's tied to the date. I think he'll wait for it. Assuming the whole thing isn't one huge mind game."

Which he wasn't going to count on, but he couldn't rule it out. He'd wondered from the very beginning how the Fishhook Rapist planned to overpower a trained FBI SWAT agent. Maybe he never planned to do that at all. Maybe he was hoping to break her from a distance.

"So then—" Maggie started.

"So nothing," Grant said. "We prepare for the worst, just in case. Let's call the rest of the team and at the very least, put them on standby."

He could tell she was in the middle of an internal debate. Finally, she conceded, "Okay, let's just text them and tell them we might need them. I don't want to call everyone out of bed on a false alarm."

"Done," Grant said. "In the meantime, we're not going

anywhere near your house. And on second thought, in case for some reason I'm on his radar, we're not going to mine. We'll go to a hotel. Even if he can find us, he won't risk getting himself caught by trying something with that many people around."

Maggie nodded slowly, her shoulders relaxing a little, but worry was still written all over her face. "That makes sense."

"Logan and Chelsie will pull through." Grant tugged her toward him until she put her arms around his back and rested her head against his chest. "You have to believe that."

"If they don't, it will be my fault."

"Bull," he said. "What happened to them was *not* your fault. And there's no way you could have predicted this. Not even Ella predicted this, and that's part of her profiling gig, figuring out what these guys will do next."

"Yeah," Maggie said, "But I should have—"

"What? Not let anyone close to you because some psycho fixated on you?" He hugged her tighter, and emotion seeped into his voice, all the worry and anger and love he was feeling right now. "Even if you'd tried, Maggie, that never would have worked. Not with Scott or Ella and not with me."

She lifted her head and told him, "Just don't get yourself shot for me again. Got it?" Her tone was lighter, as if she was trying to make a joke, but it didn't hide her concern.

"You need to stop worrying about that. It happened. It's over. And I'm fine."

As she stared up at him, looking unconvinced, she was so close, he couldn't resist. He tried to tell himself he was reassuring her as much as himself as he bent his head and brushed his lips softly over hers.

Her arms moved from his waist to his neck as she kissed him back. Unlike the previous times they'd kissed, where it quickly turned passionate and sent his libido rocketing out of control, she seemed as content as him to let their mouths linger, slow and tender.

Even after a full day in the WFO bullpen, she smelled fresh, a faintly gingery scent he associated solely with Maggie. She tasted like the best coffee he'd ever drunk, and her body fit against his with no space between them, like a puzzle piece.

When he finally eased back, the stress on her face had faded a little, and she even gave him a hesitant smile. "Let's get to that hotel."

If only circumstances were different right now, those words would have him running for the door.

She must have sensed it, because she shook her head at him, took his hand and led him into the empty parking garage.

Even though it was connected to an FBI building and there was no way Hoffmeier could have gained access, Grant's eyes swept over the open space, lingering in the dark corners, as they approached his car. Then he checked in the backseat before hustling her into the car and climbing in beside her.

"Not taking any chances," she observed, and she was glancing around the lot, too, as he put the car in gear and pulled out onto the street.

It was after midnight, but the streets were still clogged as he drove through the tourist district. He picked an expensive high-rise hotel near the Virginia border he knew had solid security, because they'd helped with the detail for a government function shortly after he'd joined the team.

Beside him, Maggie smiled approvingly as he bypassed the valet, taking a ticket and parking the car himself. They didn't have luggage, but he usually kept a duffel bag with extra clothes in the trunk, and he took the spare weaponry from his lock box and added it to the duffel.

There was no way Hoffmeier could have followed them from a nonpublic FBI building all the way to the hotel, but still, Maggie kept glancing around nervously until they'd checked in—under his name—and settled into their room on the thirtieth floor.

Grant dropped his duffel bag in the corner as Maggie sat down on the oversize chair by the floor-to-ceiling window. She kicked off her combat boots and leaned back in the chair, closing her eyes.

If it weren't for the stress radiating from her and the horrible reason they were here, this was a page out of Grant's dreams. Alone with Maggie in an absurdly decadent hotel room.

As though she could read his thoughts, her eyes opened, and she studied him. "Let me ask you something serious."

"Okay." Grant sat on the very edge of the king bed close to her, suddenly realizing it hadn't occurred to him to get a room with two beds. He hadn't even noticed it until just now.

"How can you get over what happened in that SWAT call so easily?"

"Maggie, we don't—"

"Seriously, Grant. I need to know. I mean, I'm glad it hasn't ruined things between us, believe me, but getting shot is a big deal. You just shrugged it off as though it was a blank in a training exercise."

"Well, I figure with all the crap life throws at you,

you can either choose to let it drag you down, or you can focus on the good stuff."

She leaned forward, propping her chin in her hands. "Really? And it's that easy?"

"If it's not, I hit the gym and get some sparring in. An hour in the ring kicking the heck out of a substitute—or a punching bag—also does the trick." He grinned at her.

"Now, that I can see," she said, glancing at his biceps. "So you hit the gym after that warehouse bust?"

"Nope."

She looked surprised, and maybe a little pleased, so he clarified, "Didn't need to. I meant what I said before, Maggie. You froze. It was a mistake, and an understandable one, given the situation. It was, what? Ten seconds? It just happened to be the wrong ten seconds. Honestly, I was just relieved that I got you out of the way."

She attempted a smile, but couldn't quite do it, so he added, "And then I went home and bought more stock in Kevlar."

She gave a small laugh, which he'd hoped for, and he said, "But when you asked if it was that easy? Yeah, most of the time it is. The stuff with my brothers was hard. It was so much work, every single day, trying to keep the gangs off our steps, trying to keep Ben from going to them. Not to mention just being in that house. Everything was falling apart, the rats were so bold they came out in the daytime, my mom was a mess, my dad was gone."

His shoulders tensed, remembering those days. "I spent a couple of years just mad all the time, and it got old. It probably helped with the gang stuff, and keeping my brothers in line, but it got to the point where *I* didn't like being around myself. And that's just not who I am. I'm not that pissed-off guy, angry at the world."

Maggie got up and sat beside him on the bed, leaning against him until he put his arm around her shoulder. "You do have a pretty good angry face, though," she teased.

"I do?"

"Yeah. You should see the way you glare when we go into a SWAT call. I wouldn't want to be the crook on the other side of that. This big, buff guy running toward them with an MP-5 after he's smashed the door in? No way."

"Buff, huh?"

"Like that's news," she said, nudging him. "So tell me. What happened? You got tired of being mad, so you just stopped?"

"Close enough. Things started turning around my senior year of high school. Mom got it together, got a better job. We moved somewhere a lot safer. I stopped worrying about Vinnie and Ben and started worrying about getting into college. And I just made up my mind that I might not be able to do anything about the hardships life throws at me, but I can control how I react to them."

He stopped, suddenly embarrassed. "I sound a little bit like a public service announcement, don't I?"

"Maybe a little," she joked. "But it's a good outlook. It's one of the reasons I fell for you, you know?"

His pulse picked up. "That first day I walked in to meet the SWAT team, you mean?"

She turned so he could see her clear blue eyes gazing up at him. "That's when it started." Her tone got more serious, quieter. "It's just gotten stronger."

He stared back at her, and even though he knew this was the wrong time, he couldn't help himself. "It's gotten stronger for me, too, Maggie. If I could, I'd go to the Bureau right now and tell them I can't be on your team anymore because we have a relationship that's way more than professional. If I could, I'd tell everyone I know that we'll never be able to work on the same squad again, because it would break the rules. Because I'm in love with you."

She stared at him, surprise in her eyes, and her mouth opened soundlessly.

He put his finger over her lips before she could figure out what to say. "You have other things to think about right now. I don't need you to say anything. I just wanted you to know."

She closed her eyes, as though she was working it out in her head, and he prayed he hadn't just blown it. "I realize it's too soon—"

"Shhh." She grabbed the front of his shirt and drew him toward her. She kissed him softly, twice, then leaned back to stare at him, looking so serious. Then she leaned in and pressed her lips to his once more.

Certainty flooded him in that moment. She might not feel as strongly about him, yet, but she'd already told him she'd fallen for him. He just had to give her more reasons to keep falling. And that would be easy, since he'd do anything for her.

Maybe she knew what he was thinking, because she grabbed his hand and pulled it up and around.

Realizing what she was doing, he let his hand go limp, so she could control it completely.

Her chest rose and fell faster as she placed his hand on the back of her neck, then slid her fingers down his arm until they were resting at his elbow.

He could feel the raised and puckered skin beneath his palm, but he could also feel the silky smooth skin on either side. He kept his touch light, skimming his fingers upward into the base of her hair then back down, under the edge of her blouse and back again.

She had such a soft, delicate neck, but like everything else about Maggie, there were strong muscles underneath.

Pain and anger that someone would dare do this to her flooded him, and he tried to shove it aside, because he knew it wasn't what either of them needed to focus on in this moment. Instead, he thought about what it meant for her to let him do this, and the wonder of that.

Her hand dropped off his elbow onto his knee, and she raised her head, unshed tears in her eyes as she looked at him, but with relief on her face.

He slid his hand from around the back of her neck to cup her cheek and touch his lips once more to hers, then she whispered, "I think we *are* going to have to talk to the Bureau."

It wasn't exactly a declaration of love, but it was close.

SHE WAS IN love with Grant Larkin.

She smiled and snuggled closer to him in the ridiculously huge hotel bed, feeling lighter than she had any right to feel with everything that was going on. She knew the heavy weight pressing on her would return as soon as she emerged from the dreamlike half sleep she was still in, and so she resisted wakefulness.

It wasn't hard with Grant next to her. She wasn't exactly small, but he made her feel tiny and protected. His head was barely an inch from hers on the pillow, his body seeming to somehow surround her with one hand tucked around her waist, holding her close.

Exhaustion had hit her last night so hard and fast, she'd barely gotten under the covers before falling asleep fully dressed. Apparently, Grant had shed his button-down, and the heat from his bare chest warmed her, keeping her in that sleepy haze even after she opened her eyes.

She studied his features as he slept—from the thick eyebrows, the big nose, the generous lips, to the sandpapery scruff coming in on his chin. He had a strong, hard profile, but in sleep—just like when he grinned at her in a training exercise—he didn't look intimidating.

Instead, he made her feel safe. He made her feel happy. He made her want to move forward with her life, to start a new chapter where the past no longer haunted her.

It would always be there. It had defined her for so long, in ways both good and bad. But last night, when his hands had skimmed over her neck, and all she'd felt was *Grant*, she'd realized that he was right about her. She *wasn't* broken. And she was ready for more, with him.

His eyes opened slowly, something intimate in the depths of his deep brown eyes as he smiled sleepily at her, and she knew. This was exactly how she wanted to wake up every day.

Her hands were tucked up between them, one of them clutched in his hand. She let her other hand drift down, over the bare skin of his chest, where the bruise from that bullet was just a splotch of yellow now. It was barely visible against his light brown skin. Another day or two, and it would be gone entirely.

Another day or two...

The comfortable, sleepy haze lifted, and Maggie's body tensed up. "Where'd I put my phone?"

He brought the hand resting at her waist around, and she saw he had her cell phone clutched in it. "It'd been a long day," he said, his voice rumbly with sleep. "I was worried we wouldn't hear it unless it was close."

He handed it to her, and she moved just enough to look at the readout. No missed calls. But it was earlier than she'd thought, barely 5:00 a.m. She'd only slept a few hours, and somehow she felt more rested than she had in weeks.

"I should call the hospital, check on Logan and Chelsie."

When she just stared at the phone, not moving, Grant asked, "You want me to make the call?"

"No." Chelsie was supposedly stable. And whatever Logan's status right now, Ella deserved to hear from her. "I can do it."

Before she could dial, the phone rang, startling her.

The readout just read "Private Number." Probably the hospital. "How are they?" she answered.

"They?" a voice came over the phone that locked her muscles and sent fear racing through her.

She must have looked panicked, because Grant leaned in close, propping up on one elbow and leaning down so he could hear, too.

Her hands trembled, but she turned the volume up and tilted the phone a little so he could listen.

"You mean *her*, don't you?" that voice from her nightmares continued. "Or are you talking about Logan and Chelsie? Tsk, tsk."

"What do you want, Hoffmeier?" Maggie demanded, and her voice came out stronger than she'd expected as Grant took her hand in his.

There was a pause, then he responded, "You figured that out, did you?" A hint of unease sounded in his voice, but it was gone when he said, "Too bad you didn't figure out my plan sooner, isn't it?"

"You're not going to get away with this," Maggie said, wondering how he'd even gotten her cell phone number. Was he close?

She couldn't help looking at the huge window across from the bed, behind Grant. The thick, heavy curtains were drawn, no way for Hoffmeier to get line of sight if he was across the street peering down a rifle scope.

Hoffmeier laughed, a nasty, ugly sound that seemed

to skitter over her skin, making her feel dirty. "I already have."

"What are you talking about?" she asked, her dread swelling. Had Logan died?

"You have forty minutes," he told her, his voice eerily calm and confident as he gave her an address that sounded vaguely familiar.

"His parents' country house," Grant mouthed.

"You come to me, alone," Hoffmeier said.

She wanted to laugh back at him, to scoff and call his bluff, except he sounded too confident, too certain she'd agree. And she knew, deep in her gut, that he'd found a way to win again.

"Aren't you going to ask why you'd do that?" he mocked.

Grant's jaw tightened, and Maggie could tell it was taking everything in him to stay quiet, to let Hoffmeier believe she was alone right now.

"Why?" she asked, and her voice shook.

"Because I have something you want."

There was a brief shuffling noise, then her sister's voice came over the line, high-pitched, scared and speaking at warp speed. "I'm so sorry, Maggie. I came to DC, anyway. I knocked on your door, and you weren't home and then I was on my way back to the hotel and he grabbed me. I didn't—"

"That's enough," Hoffmeier said, and Nikki was gone.

Maggie sucked in a breath that didn't seem to contain nearly enough oxygen and choked out, "Leave her alone! I'll be there, I promise. Just please don't hurt her."

"Come alone," he repeated. "I even *think* you have backup, and she's dead. *After* I give her a token on her neck to match yours."

Maggie's hand tightened around the phone, panicked

for the baby sister she'd always tried to protect from this evil. "Don't touch her," she barked, terrified that it was too late.

"Forty minutes," he reminded her, then hung up.

Chapter Fifteen

"Hang on," Grant said as Maggie leaped out of the bed, tangling in the covers and almost pitching herself to the floor.

She righted herself, tossed him her phone and ran for her boots, lacing them up fast. "Look up the address, would you? Get me directions." She checked her watch, and there was panic in her voice when she choked out, "Forty minutes! I can't make it in forty minutes, not even if I speed the whole way."

Grant pulled his shirt on, punching the address into her phone as he groped for his own shoes with his other hand. "Just wait a second, Maggie. Let's call Clive, have him get the rest of the team on the move."

"There's no time! That's the whole point. They can't gear up and get out there that fast, either. And it's in the middle of nowhere, that much I know. We have no time for a tactical plan, and he'd see them coming from a mile away. This is Nikki's life. I'm not risking it."

"Maggie," Grant pressed. "We train for this."

She strapped on her holster, then raced over to his duffel bag, unzipping it. Ignoring his comment, she asked, "You have an ankle holster? Something I can take as a backup?"

"Nothing that won't show," he said. "But I'm your backup."

"No," she answered, the way he'd known she would. She was in full-on panic mode, desperate and not thinking straight.

He yanked his shoes on, then hurried to her side and grabbed her arm, making her pause.

"Grant, I have to *go.*"

"Just hang on a second, okay? You can't run right into his trap. That's going to get both you and Nikki hurt."

She froze at his words, and her arm tensed under his hold.

"It's going to be okay," he reassured her, but she shook her head.

"I don't think it is," she whispered. "I have to play by his rules. I can't let him do to Nikki what…what he did to me."

It was unspoken, but hung in the air, that it might already be too late.

"We need to treat this like a SWAT call," he said, trying to reason with her, but the truth was, they *didn't* have a lot of options. Not on that timetable, and not with the location he'd provided.

Even if they called the rest of the team, the houses—estates, really—where the Hoffmeier family had their second home was deep in Virginia horse country, where neighbors were miles apart. Worse, land there was flat enough to see for miles. The team would only be able to drive in so far, and they'd have to hoof it from there. By the time they arrived unseen, it would probably be too late.

Still, if everything fell apart, it would be good to know they were on the way.

Maggie stepped back and yanked her blouse down

over her gun, her movements jerky and panicked. "I'll call them on the way."

"Okay." He strapped on his own Glock, then took out his MP-5. He dumped out the contents of his duffel, then stuffed the gun back in, zipping it up. "But I'm going with you."

Her head swiveled toward the door and back, desperation still in her eyes, her body twitching with her obvious need to move. "You heard him—"

"I'm not a full SWAT team. It'll be easier for me to sneak in with you."

She shook her head. "I have to *go*."

"Fine. We can argue on the way," he said. "Let's move."

"WATCH THE LIGHT," Grant warned.

Instead of stopping as the light at the intersection turned from green to yellow, Maggie slapped Grant's siren on the roof of his car and flew through it. Honking and the squeal of tires filled the air, and she just pushed down on the gas, taking the corners dangerously fast.

She called on every bit of the special defensive driving training she'd taken at the FBI's training facility at Quantico as she raced through the outskirts of DC. It wasn't even 6:00 a.m. yet, but here, commuters were already out, ladder-climbers getting an early start, and political assistants prepping for the day ahead.

"You can't stay there once we get close," Maggie said, keeping her attention totally on the road, watching the sidewalks in her peripheral vision for jaywalkers.

Panic threatened, like a river about to burst through a levee. How had he gotten close enough to her house to spot Nikki? And how had no one noticed Nikki had left Indiana for DC?

Sitting beside her, Grant said, "When we're close, I'm going to get down in the backseat."

"He'll see you!"

"No, he won't," Grant replied, sounding calm. "You'll stop the car far enough away. He's not going to be looking in the backseat. To do that, he'd have to get close enough to have his back to you, and he's not stupid. He's going to make you come to him. So you leave me in the car. I'll come after you."

There was such confidence in his voice, such certainty. She'd heard it plenty of times in SWAT calls, and he'd always been able to back it up. But today was different, in so many ways.

"Maybe you should just get out before we drive close enough for him to see the car," Maggie suggested. She knew the area where Hoffmeier had called her to was nothing but open spaces and gently rolling hills. For her to stop where he couldn't see the car would be too far away for Grant to help.

"No," Grant replied. "But that's where Clive will be."

"Don't call Clive," she burst when Grant started to dial his phone. "Hoffmeier knows what I do. What if he's sending me here as a test? What if he's not there at all? I could show up and find a note on the door, sending me to some other property his parents own under that shell company. Meanwhile, he's got a camera set up there and knows I've brought backup and he kills Nikki!"

"That's really elaborate," Grant reasoned. "Most criminals think basic."

"Well, it was pretty elaborate to hire a druggie to break into Scott's house and shoot Chelsie. It was pretty elaborate to hire a couple of guys to open fire into a crime scene with police detectives there. Who knows who else he's hired? Who knows who else he's got with him, watching the area!"

"Your sister said she came to DC on her own. She couldn't have been here long, which means this wasn't his original plan. Not this part. So he's working at least a little bit on the fly here. He hasn't had a lot of time to work all the details out."

"Yeah, but this guy has gotten away with it for a decade! He's not stupid." Maggie whipped around another tight corner, then finally, finally, she was on the I-66 West freeway heading out of DC. It was an hour's drive to the location he'd named, in the best traffic conditions. Even speeding like a maniac, she wasn't sure she'd make it in Hoffmeier's forty-minute time line.

She knew that was the point. He wanted to give her no time to react, no time to come up with a counterplan. He wanted to make her panic, so she wasn't thinking clearly when she arrived. So he'd have the upper hand.

It was working.

"No, Hoffmeier isn't stupid," Grant agreed, still sounding calm; he might've been in the WFO office, planning SWAT details. "But his goal is to get you there. And I bet those guys he hired were purely about throwing cash at people who already had records. There's no way he'd invite strangers into this part. This is about him. And it's about you. He's counting on you to react emotionally."

"I know," she told Grant. "But what choice do I have? This isn't just another SWAT call. This is my sister. I'm not taking any chances."

"Our team is the best," Grant said, still sounding way too calm, as he put the phone to his ear. Then she heard him talking to Clive, going over the details, warning Clive to stay at a distance until they'd checked the place out.

The truth was, Clive and the team wouldn't make it until past the deadline, anyway. The hotel had been a solid twenty minutes closer to Virginia than Clive and her other teammates, who lived on the opposite side of DC. By then, she'd know for sure if Hoffmeier's plan was more involved than it seemed, if he was planning to send her somewhere else. By then, she'd have eyes on Nikki. By then, hopefully, it would all be over.

If it wasn't, there was a good chance she'd need the team. She couldn't risk bringing them too early and alerting him, but thinking like a civilian and playing entirely by his rules could get everyone hurt. She had to have a contingency plan in place, and besides Grant, Scott and Ella, she trusted her SWAT team the most. If she didn't make it, she wanted Nikki safe.

Before she knew it, Grant had put his phone back in his pocket. "The team is coming," he said calmly as she picked up her speed even more. "It's going to be okay."

She bit back her instant response. There was no reason to take out her fear and anger on him, not when he was putting his life in danger for her and Nikki. Not when she cared about him the way she did.

What if she never got the chance to tell him?

"Grant, I need to tell you…" She took a deep breath, wishing she could actually look at him when she said she loved him for the first time. But she couldn't. She was going ninety-five on the freeway, racing around the other vehicles with her siren blaring.

"Tell me later," Grant said, and from the tone of his voice, she could tell he knew it was about their budding relationship.

"But just in case—"

"You don't need a *just in case*. We're both coming out of this, and you can tell me when your sister is safe, okay?"

"Okay," she said, because right now, she needed both of their attention focused on saving Nikki.

But the words sat heavy on her tongue. She prayed he was right, and she would get the chance to say them.

The reality was, she'd do whatever it took to get Nikki away from Hoffmeier. And if she had to trade her own life to do it, she wouldn't hesitate.

Her hands gripped the wheel even tighter, and the farther they got from DC, the lighter the traffic got, giving her room to increase her speed even more. Beside her, Grant had one hand braced on the door handle, but he didn't say a word as she picked it up to over a hundred miles an hour.

He got his duffel bag from the backseat and removed his MP-5, then crammed the empty duffel under the front seat. He set the MP-5 in the backseat, where he'd be climbing before too long.

"You have any other weapons?" she asked, even though she shouldn't need them. Chances were, Hoffmeier would try to get her to lay her gun down. But all she needed to do was get close enough. Her training with the FBI's SWAT team meant her hands were deadly weapons. Assuming she didn't freeze the way she had in the warehouse the second she saw Hoffmeier with her sister.

"I've got the obvious," Grant said. "Wrench for changing a tire, pen knife."

"Pen knife," Maggie said. "Can you put it in my pocket?"

Grant reached into the glove box and took out a small folding knife, then slid it into the pocket of her slacks. "He'll probably search you."

"He gets that close, and I won't need the knife," Maggie said darkly, praying it was true. Praying that if she got the chance to pull her Glock on him, her trigger finger wouldn't shake the way her entire body did every time she so much as thought about seeing Hoffmeier face-to-face.

"That's my girl."

"You're right about that," she said seriously, taking her eyes off the road for just a second to look his way, hoping he understood the subtext. He wanted her to wait to tell him she loved him, fine. But at least this way, if the worst happened, he'd know.

He squeezed her knee as she took the exit onto M-50 and glanced at the dashboard clock. If she could keep her speed up on the country highway, they might actually make it.

Just as that thought hit, Grant's phone rang.

"It's Clive," Grant said, picking it up and talking to their team leader a minute. Then he told her, "I'm leaving the call open," and he stuffed the phone under the middle seat. "He'll be able to hear us," Grant explained to her. "If he has to, he can call HRT, and they can come in by helicopter."

Maggie nodded mutely. If Chelsie hadn't been shot, Scott would have been with HRT right now, armed with a sniper rifle that could take out Hoffmeier from half a mile away. All assuming he'd have been able to mobilize and find an unseen location by then, and assuming Hoffmeier came out into the open.

But the deeper into the country they traveled, the more she realized how smart Hoffmeier had been in choosing his location. A distance shot wasn't going to happen here.

If he was going to be taken down, it would have to happen up close. And she was the only one who'd be able to get close enough without endangering Nikki.

"This is the road," she finally said, terror settling

deep inside as she followed the GPS onto a smaller country road.

The scenery was gorgeous: deep green, rolling plains dotted with grazing horses and the occasional estate. It was also the perfect place to hide a kidnap victim. Even if a scream echoed here, who would hear it?

"I'm getting in the back now," Grant said.

She slowed her speed a little as Grant unfastened his seat belt and climbed into the backseat, settling down on the floor, where there was no way Hoffmeier would see him without standing close to the car. She glanced over her shoulder and saw he had one hand lingering near the holster, holding his Glock, and his MP-5 clutched in his other hand.

"Here we go," she said, turning onto a driveway so long it could have been its own private road. She slowed even more, rolling down her windows so she could hear as she passed large, empty fields meant for horses.

She studied two huge outbuildings as she drove past, but continued on toward the looming main house straight ahead. It was ridiculously ornate, lined with perfectly groomed shrubbery, columns highlighting the entryway. An empty truck was right up front.

Maggie squinted at the house, still a solid five hundred feet away up the drive. "I don't see him," she whispered.

The boom of a voice—*Hoffmeier's* voice—startled her so badly she jerked the wheel, almost veering off the drive.

He was using a bullhorn, she realized, even though she still didn't see him. But he was here.

"Stop the car," he ordered, so she did, planting her foot on the brake, but not putting the car in park.

Her hands shook around the wheel as she waited for more, as she squinted at the house, trying to see any sign of where he was. Something glinted in a front window, and she stared until her eyes hurt, but she couldn't tell what it was.

"Toss your gun out the window," he said, and his voice made the nerve endings in her neck fire to life, almost as if they were preparing for the pain of another brand.

When she hesitated, he snapped, "Don't make me ask again."

Maggie undid her seat belt and unholstered her Glock, holding it out the window so he could see, then dropped it.

"Good," he said, sounding pleased and confident, as if he'd always known it would come back to this, to him in charge. "Now, your backup weapon."

She held up her hands and shook her head, assuming he was staring at her through binoculars.

"Of course you brought a backup gun," he said. "Let's motivate you."

A pained scream echoed through the bullhorn, bringing tears to Maggie's eyes, and Grant's whisper barely penetrated her fear.

"Under the seat."

Reaching down, she picked up his Glock, then held it out the window and tossed it as tears tracked down her cheeks. She didn't bother to wipe them away. He wanted to be in charge, and as much as everything in her resisted, she needed to show him he was. She needed to let him think this would break her. Needed to get him to let her close enough to bring him down. Her hands clenched into tight fists on her lap, where he couldn't see them.

"Very good," Hoffmeier said, and there was that flicker again, in the front window.

Was it open? Maggie wondered.

"Now there's just one more thing," Hoffmeier continued, "and then you can drive up to the house. You follow all my instructions, and I'll let Nikki walk out of here. You know it isn't her I want."

Maggie stared at the house, her jaw trembling, and not because she was trying to let him see fear, but because she couldn't control it. Because she knew exactly who he did want. And she knew exactly what he wanted from her.

"You don't follow my instructions, and I'll shoot her right now, you understand?"

All she could do was nod desperately and wait.

"Tell Grant to get out of the car," his voice boomed.

Maggie froze, terror lodging in her throat. What was he going to do to Grant if she told him to do it? What was he going to do to Nikki if she didn't?

"Tick tock," Hoffmeier mocked.

Before Maggie could figure out what to do, she heard the back car door open.

"Grant, don't," she warned, and her voice came out a desperate whisper, but she was too late.

A flash of light exploded at the front window, with a sharp crack that sent birds flapping from a grove of trees behind the house. Next to her car, Grant dropped to the ground, and dark red spread across his chest.

"Now you can come get Nikki," Hoffmeier said, opening the front door and stepping outside, a pistol pointed at her sister's head.

Chapter Sixteen

"Grant!" Maggie cried, her foot automatically lifting off the brake. The car rolled forward, and she stamped her foot back down, glancing over her shoulder. "Grant," she pleaded again through the open window.

On the ground, Grant lay flat on his back with his right arm splayed out beside him, completely still, not responding. Maggie knew the amount of blood seeping through his shirt meant if he wasn't already dead, he would be soon.

Panic raced through her, the desire to leap out of the car and check his vitals. To press her hands into the wound and try to stop the bleeding.

"Tick tock," Hoffmeier called, startling her.

She looked back at him, where he held a bullhorn in one hand and Nikki in front of him. Then she glanced once more at Grant and gulped back a sob. This time, he wasn't wearing any Kevlar. This time, there would be no "do overs."

"Now!" Hoffmeier screamed. "Or Nikki pays, too!"

Praying Grant was still alive—and that Clive had heard them over the open phone line in the car and was coming—Maggie pressed on the gas, stopping right in front of the porch.

Up close, she could see that Nikki's hands were bound

together in front of her. She was wearing shorts and a T-shirt, and although she was clearly terrified, she was alert, and Maggie didn't see any obvious injuries. She hoped there were none she couldn't see, no brand already seared into Nikki's neck.

Nikki's lips moved, and although Maggie couldn't quite hear her, she read the words. "I'm so sorry."

Hoffmeier dropped the bullhorn on the ground, drawing her attention to him. He looked older than the pictures she'd seen of him, and the years hadn't treated him well. If the idea that people's psychology eventually showed up on their faces was true, he was a prime example.

He still had the good bone structure, but there were more lines on his face than he should have had at his age. The smug, vile smirk that looked stamped on his face overrode any charm he might have once possessed.

But he was still in good physical shape. Maybe more so than he'd been a decade ago, judging by the muscle outlined on his bare arms. Even if she could get close, he wouldn't go down easily.

"Get out of the car, slowly," Hoffmeier said, "and don't try anything."

She turned off the engine and stepped out, her hands up over her head, an overriding fury surging inside.

He waved the hand holding the gun at her, and Maggie's calves tensed the second his weapon left Nikki's temple, but he was too far away to rush.

His eyes narrowed, and he pressed the gun back to her sister's head before he demanded, "Lift your shirt. Are you wearing a holster?"

Every time he spoke, she had to resist the urge to cower. Even with him right in front of her, no flashbacks raced forward, but his voice was imprinted on her memory like a brand of its own.

"Yes. For the gun you made me toss." Her voice came out shaky, and she moved slowly, lifting the side of her blouse so he could see her holster was empty. The weight of the pen knife in her pocket seemed abnormally heavy, and she hunched a little, hoping he couldn't tell she had something there.

"Good," he said, not seeming to notice. "Let's go inside, then." His tone was suddenly jovial, as if he was inviting her to brunch. He backed toward the house, dragging Nikki inside with him.

Her sister's gaze locked on hers as she was yanked inside, such guilt and regret there, the same things Maggie felt herself whenever she thought about the Fishhook Rapist.

She cast one more desperate glance over her shoulder, but in the distance, she could see that Grant was still prone on the ground.

She looked farther down the road, but there were no SWAT vehicles barreling down on them. She needed them right now, for Grant. Yet, if they showed up, Hoffmeier would surely kill Nikki.

Her vision clouded with tears, Maggie followed them inside.

Hoffmeier and Nikki backed through a long entryway into a formal living room, and Maggie walked a few paces behind, her hands up by her ears. The second she entered the room, her eyes were drawn to the elaborate painting on the wall, inside a gilded frame. Then they were pulled to the antique coffee table with the ball and claw feet and the beautiful marble top.

The place where he'd forced her to her knees and branded the back of her neck, tying them together forever. On top of the table was a circular piece of metal attached to a short pole, and as Maggie squinted at it, she realized what it was. A modified family crest, one hook soldered to raise above the rest.

Her whole body shuddered, and Hoffmeier's lips slowly spread. "You remember," he whispered.

This is going to hurt. This is going to hurt. This is going to hurt.

The words chanted like a record set too fast that she couldn't turn off, until she wanted to curl into a ball and slap her hands over her ears. Only it wouldn't help, because the voice was in her head.

"I hoped someday you'd remember what we had," he said, and Nikki suddenly stiffened and snapped, "Stop it!"

Hoffmeier drew the pistol away from her temple then slapped it across her cheek, making Nikki's head whip sideways and blood trickle from her lip.

It snapped the world into focus for Maggie, and she straightened her spine. "I'm here. Time to let Nikki go."

Her voice sounded stronger, and Hoffmeier's smile faded. "Not yet. I know what you do for the FBI, Maggie."

He shifted to the side, yanking Nikki with him, and behind them, Maggie realized there were two mahogany chairs in the middle of the room. "A place for us to talk," he told her. "You sit in the one on the right. There are ties there to make sure you do as you're told."

"Don't do it," Nikki burst out.

Maggie shook her head at her sister, willing her not to antagonize him. "What assurance do I have you'll let Nikki go once I do what you want?"

His eyebrows lifted. "You'll just have to trust me. What choice do you have? Don't do what I say, and I pull the trigger." He tapped the gun barrel against Nikki's head.

"And then I kill you," Maggie vowed, her voice dark and so ominous even Nikki's eyes widened.

"Oh, I probably won't shoot her in the head," Hoffmeier said conversationally. "But a kneecap maybe. Somewhere really painful, that'll never heal right."

He swept his free hand grandly toward the chair, as though he was presenting something at auction, and Maggie moved slowly toward it.

If she could just get close enough, get him to lift his gun away from her sister's head...

But as she stepped toward them, Hoffmeier yanked Nikki off to the side, away from the chairs. So they were both out of striking range.

Nikki mouthed, *No.* But what choice did she have? Maggie picked the zip ties off the chair and sat down.

"Loop it around your wrist and the chair arm," Hoffmeier instructed. "Hurry up."

It was awkward, but Maggie managed to get one arm fastened to the chair, then she held up her free hand with the other zip tie and shook her head. "I can't do this with one hand."

"That's okay," he said cheerfully. "Nikki will finish it." His tone turned menacing. "And you'll sit still. If I could hit your boyfriend in the heart from five hundred feet, I can hit your sister in the head from three." He smiled, a crazy glee in his eyes as he added, "Dad taught me to shoot skeet when I was five, but it never interested me until recently."

Pain wrenched through her at the mention of Grant, and Maggie pushed it aside. She had to focus on Nikki now.

She had to watch for any chance to escape, because yes, Hoffmeier really wanted her. So he might well just let Nikki go once he had her immobilized. By the time

Nikki could get help, he could plan to knock Maggie out with something, load her in the trunk and be long gone.

Yet it was equally likely he'd keep Nikki right here, use her to make Maggie tame, to get her to do whatever he wanted.

Maggie tried to numb herself, tried not to think about what he might want, as Nikki approached. Maggie kept her eyes on Hoffmeier, looking for any moment that his gun might move away from Nikki. If she had the chance, it didn't matter that the chair was attached to her wrist. She'd bring it with her when she tackled him. It was awkward, but it weighed less than her fifty pounds of SWAT gear.

Nikki reached her side, and her own hands, already tied together so tight her wrists were raw, fumbled with the second zip tie. Her fingers trembled as she closed the zip tie around Maggie's other wrist. The whole time, Hoffmeier just stared back at her, barely blinking, his bottomless blue gaze unnerving.

"You okay?" Maggie whispered, and Nikki nodded.

"Enough sisterly love," Hoffmeier said. "Take the other seat, Nikki."

"No," Maggie burst. "Let her go!"

"I will," Hoffmeier said, then waved Nikki over. "Eventually. Right now, I need her here to keep you in line. I know you, Maggie," he purred. "You were always a fighter."

She wrenched at the ties, bile rising up in her throat. She didn't remember the assault; did that mean she'd fought him back then? Or was he just referring to her using his attack as motivation to join SWAT?

Nikki's head moved back and forth between them. "Leave my sister alone."

"Listen to that," Hoffmeier said. "I guess Nikki here

is getting a backbone. I like that in a woman." He sighed dramatically. "Too bad for her that I'm already way too obsessed with her big sister to bother with the knockoff version."

Maggie scowled at him, then glanced at Nikki and hoped she wasn't making an irreversible mistake. "Do what he says." Instinct told her he would only hurt Nikki to force her hand, that he was being honest about wanting to hurt Maggie, not her sister.

"No," Nikki said, and her jaw jutted out as she stepped in front of Maggie. "My sister has her team of SWAT agents on the way and they're going to—"

"Now!" Hoffmeier bellowed.

"Nikki, please. Just do it," Maggie begged, and with one last worried glance at her, Nikki sat in the other chair.

Hoffmeier kept his gun aimed at her, and he stayed carefully away from Maggie as he walked to the far side and secured an extra zip tie to the one around Nikki's wrists, so she was latched to the second chair.

Only then did he turn his gun on Maggie and move closer, murmuring, "I've been waiting so long for this."

Maggie fought off the panic building inside her and prepared herself. Keep coming, she willed him, hoping that if he gave her the chance, she wouldn't freeze up.

But the nearer he got, the faster her breath came, the louder her heartbeat thudded in her eardrums, the more terror clouded her vision. Was this the end for her and Nikki both?

GRANT GROANED AND rolled to his left, uninjured side, trying to push himself off the dirt. His right arm hung limply at his side, blood dripping steadily down it.

He'd waited until Hoffmeier had disappeared inside with Maggie and Nikki to try to move at all, not wanting

Hoffmeier to realize he'd survived. The way his shoulder throbbed and pumped blood, that survival was still in question.

Fighting dizziness as he got to his knees, Grant managed to get his button-down off. He swore as he slid the shirt off his damaged right arm and got a good look at the injury.

As a SWAT agent, he had basic medical training, the sort of thing a soldier learned for the battlefield. But he didn't need it to know his injury was bad. Really bad.

His shirt was soaked through with blood, and so was the ground below him. He had to stop the flow, or he was going to die of blood loss way before backup arrived.

Awkwardly, he managed to wrap the shirt around his shoulder, getting it above the bullet hole. Using his good hand and his teeth, he tugged the knot tight enough that the blood slowed to a stop.

His right hand immediately started to tingle and as he pushed himself to his feet, he swayed and almost fell. Realizing he didn't have a weapon anymore, Grant stumbled as he looked around, finally spotting his Glock a few feet away in the dirt. He walked unsteadily over to it, a wave of dizziness sweeping through him as he bent down to grab it off the ground.

His hand shook around the handle, and he knew the gun wasn't going to do him any good. His body was already shutting down from the blood loss. The likelihood of being able to pull the trigger with Hoffmeier standing close to either Maggie or Nikki and actually hitting Hoffmeier wasn't strong.

Nerves rose up, for Maggie, for Nikki, for himself, and he tried to think the way he would on a SWAT call. Stay calm and focus.

He shoved the gun in his holster, clenched his teeth

against the pain and headed for his car, up by the house. If he could just get to the cell phone, he could tell Clive to call HRT, get them airborne immediately. If he was really, really lucky, Clive and the rest of their team were already close, and they'd arrive in time to stop Hoffmeier from carrying out whatever plan he had for Maggie and Nikki.

New pinpricks of pain skittered up his arm as it began reacting to the blood flow being cut off. It meant he'd successfully tied off the wound, which would buy him some time, but it also meant that arm was completely useless.

Reaching the car, Grant braced himself against it. He reached for the door handle, then moved his hand away. He'd have to get down on the floor and reach under the seat to search for the phone, and if he bent back down, there was a good chance he wouldn't get up again.

Normally, Grant would have skirted the front entry of the house and moved around the side, peering into the windows and getting a lock on the subject and the hostages before he made a move. But with Maggie inside and knowing his time of being any help at all was fading fast, he climbed onto the porch and looked into the house. The door was open, and he could see a long, ornate entryway, but not Maggie or Nikki. Not Hoffmeier.

He had to get to Maggie now, while there was still something he might be able to do. Hopefully, she wouldn't even need him, but since he'd come up close to the house, he hadn't heard anything from inside.

He was careful with every step because he was feeling clumsy from blood loss, and he didn't want to stumble, make noise and give himself away. But fear skyrocketed as Maggie's anguished voice screamed out, "You said you wanted me! Leave her alone!"

Flattening himself against the wall, and vaguely registering that he was smearing it with blood, Grant peered around the corner and into the large living room. At the far end of the room, Hoffmeier had his back to Grant. Maggie and Nikki were each tied to a chair in front of him. Hoffmeier was leaning toward Nikki, running the hand not clutching his gun over her face, but his attention was entirely on Maggie.

Maggie's eyes suddenly widened, and he realized she'd spotted him. He ducked his head back around the corner just in case her reaction gave away his presence.

Dizziness hit again, and he closed his eyes briefly. Was he going to be able to help, or would he just get them all hurt?

Grant willed his body to hold out a little longer and carefully peeked around the corner again. There was no way he could use a gun right now, but he didn't need his arm for pure, brute force. He tried to signal Maggie, but had no idea if she knew what he was telling her.

"I don't want her," Hoffmeier told Maggie. "And now that you're here—" he gestured to her, tied up in the chair "—I don't need her."

Instead of the terror Hoffmeier had probably expected to see on Maggie's face, fury raced over her features. "What do you want?" she barked. "I'm here. But it sure seems like you're too scared to get close, even with me tied up."

"Maggie," Nikki whispered, but Maggie ignored her, her eyes lasered in on Hoffmeier.

Grant couldn't see his face, but his whole body visibly stiffened. "I didn't think you'd have figured out my name, but it was going to come out. It was always going to come out. I had everything planned out perfectly," he bragged, his gun hand drifting down as he talked to Maggie.

Although Maggie just continued glaring, Grant knew

her. She was waiting for him to get more distracted, to move the gun a little bit more away from Nikki.

"Your sister doesn't matter. She wasn't even part of the original plan, but she sure did make it easier when she showed up at your door. She really looks like you, you know? I was just going to leave her here, tied up, until someone came and got her. She would have been fine, but she's unimportant. Expendable, if you didn't follow my instructions, if I needed her to make you behave. Your boyfriend doesn't matter, either, although him I kind of wanted to kill. You belong to me!" He bellowed the last part.

"After ten years, I knew it was time. The perfect time." He laughed. "I never actually planned to wait until the first to come for you, but I needed you to believe that. We were going to have two perfect days together, and then I was going to call your brother on the first, tell him where to find us. On our anniversary."

In that instant, Grant realized the rest of Hoffmeier's plan. From the look on Maggie's face, so did she. This was his end game.

"We were going to be together forever, Maggie," Hoffmeier purred, and he moved a little more, obviously wanting to revel in Maggie's reaction to that news.

It was a huge mistake. And Grant knew Maggie. He knew she would take advantage of that error.

So the second he saw it, he didn't wait for her signal. He just raced as hard and as fast as he could into the room.

He watched Maggie's feet shoot out and lock around Hoffmeier's knees the instant he moved the gun off Nikki. She used her legs to yank him down hard.

Hoffmeier flew backward, his arms lurching up, and

his head smacked the floor as the gun blasted a hole in the ceiling, dumping plaster on top of him.

Tied up, Maggie didn't get her feet clear fast enough, and her chair slammed down, too, rolling sideways, right after Hoffmeier. He swore and swung his gun back around fast, looking furious and only a little disoriented from the fall.

Grant had a brief vision of Nikki uselessly fighting her bonds, of Maggie scrambling to right herself, before he pushed off and dived the final distance straight at Hoffmeier.

Chapter Seventeen

Grant landed on top of Hoffmeier, and he heard the air whoosh out of Hoffmeier's lungs. Then the gun blasted off again, with deafening effects, right beside Grant's ear.

His right shoulder screamed in pain as Grant reared back and smashed his left fist into the space between Hoffmeier's shoulder and his chest. Hoffmeier's eyes went wide with pain, but the gun didn't fall, so Grant hit again, swallowing back nausea at the movement.

This time, the gun dropped out of Hoffmeier's hand, but Hoffmeier got smart and twisted underneath Grant, smashing his own fist into Grant's wounded arm.

Searing pain raced down his arm and across his chest, and he was pretty sure something in his shoulder tore. Trying to ignore it, Grant flung his right arm wide, knocking Hoffmeier's pistol out of reach.

Blackness threatened at the edges of his vision, and something damp that had to be blood escaping his makeshift tourniquet splattered like big raindrops onto Hoffmeier. He willed his body to keep going, to stay conscious long enough to get rid of the threat, to get Maggie free.

Beside him, on the ground, he could hear Maggie frantically trying to get her arms unhooked from the chair, without success. Then she seemed to give up on it and just spun, pushing the chair backward so her feet were pointed toward him.

Grant used his good arm to propel himself up off Hoffmeier enough to give her a target, and she didn't hesitate. His whole body was wrenched sideways along with Hoffmeier as Maggie kicked up and out, meeting Hoffmeier's chin with her foot.

The strike effectively knocked both of them out of her reach, but it slowed Hoffmeier down, and Grant pushed up to his knees, trying to get another hit in.

Before he could, Hoffmeier recovered, shoving Grant off him. He scrambled to his feet, glanced at the gun in the corner, then back at Grant, who was hauling himself up on Nikki's chair.

It felt as if Grant was moving in slow motion, inch by painful inch, but he must still have seemed like a threat to Hoffmeier as he finally hauled himself to his feet.

Because instead of running for the gun, Hoffmeier glanced desperately at Maggie one last time, then swore and ran the other way, out the door.

"Grant! Grant!" Maggie sobbed.

He was staring in the direction Hoffmeier had disappeared, but it wasn't until he looked back at her that her fear subsided. His arm looked bad, but when Hoffmeier had hit him and the wound had opened up again, she'd thought he was going down for good.

He looked steadier on his feet now, and his shoulder had stopped bleeding. "How hurt are you?" she asked.

"I'll make it," he said, and dropped to his knees beside her.

"I didn't know if you—" she started.

"I know," he said, and his words slurred a little, then

he seemed to make a conscious effort to sharpen them. "I'm sorry. I couldn't let Hoffmeier see I was alive."

"My pocket," she said, moving closer so he could get access. "The knife."

"Got it," he said, and fumbled for it, finally getting the knife out and open.

As he cut awkwardly at the zip tie, she studied his face, looking for signs he was worse than he was telling her. Then she glanced at Nikki, still tied to the chair, who had silent tears running down her face.

"You okay?" Maggie asked.

"I'm fine," Nikki answered. "He didn't hurt me, he just hit me the one time to make me scream when…" She choked back tears. "I'm so sorry. And then he fired the rifle and…"

"It's okay," Grant told her. "I'm tougher than I look."

Nikki actually laughed a little through her tears, probably because Grant looked pretty tough. Then she stared at Maggie. "Are *you* okay?"

"I'm fine," Maggie said. It was Grant she was worried about. And Hoffmeier getting away, disappearing for another decade.

As soon as Grant got the zip ties sliced open, Maggie lurched for the landline, knowing that Grant needed help soon. Instead of calling an ambulance, she called Clive. "Where are you?"

"Two minutes out, max," he answered.

"Go faster," she begged. "Grant needs medical attention now. He was shot, and I need you to get him airlifted out of here to the closest hospital."

"I'll make it," Grant told her, giving her a weary-looking smile as he shuffled over to her sister on his knees and set the pen knife against her zip ties.

"Where's Hoffmeier?" Clive asked.

"He ran." She glanced at Grant, cutting her sister free, and then at the doorway. Could she wait for Clive? Or would Hoffmeier get away again? With his resources, would they ever find him?

She looked at the marble coffee table where he'd pressed her head a decade ago, and at the metal brand he'd made, still lying there.

Would he get away again, make a new brand? Keep trying to punish his family for their perceived wrongs against him? Keep hurting young women, to try and give himself some kind of sick power?

"Go," Grant said. "Get him. End this for good."

Over the phone, Clive said, "Here we come. We're at the drive."

"Go now," Grant said. "Don't let Hoffmeier get away."

The squeal of tires sounded outside, and Maggie jumped to her feet. She heard Grant's voice call after her, "Be careful," as she ran as fast as her feet would carry her out the door.

The living room opened up on the other side into an expansive kitchen, and the back door was hanging open. Maggie might have thought it was a trick, except the wide, flat land that had been a challenge before was now a benefit. She spotted him, running flat-out across the expansive field behind the house, away from the SWAT agents' vehicles descending on the front where his truck was parked.

He glanced back at her, and in that instant she realized she'd left her gun behind, that it was just her and Hoffmeier again. The way it was ten years ago.

She pushed down her emotional reaction and tried to think like the SWAT agent she'd become. She had the upper hand this time.

She took off as fast as she could after him, her combat

boots smashing through the thick, immaculately groomed grass. Her lungs burned as she pushed herself harder, and the distance between them began to close.

He looked back again, stumbled when he saw how close she was getting, and then turned, heading in the other direction, around the back of the house, toward an enormous man-made pond.

Maggie followed, and just as Hoffmeier looked as if he was going to change direction again, Maggie realized she was close enough. She pushed off and flew through the air toward him, landing hard and taking him down with her.

They crashed into the muddy ground at the edge of the pond, Maggie on Hoffmeier's back, and she scrambled to get to her knees. To push him down flat and get his arms behind his back. It occurred to her in that moment that she'd left her handcuffs back in the hotel room, but it didn't matter, because he suddenly flipped over, getting her beneath him.

"It's not finished," he panted, sounding out of breath and injured.

He was heavier than he looked, and with the back of his head pressed against her face, Maggie got a whiff of his expensive cologne, and it took her back ten years. The same smell, the same voice, the same man.

Instead of immobilizing her, it filled her with fury. "Yes, it is," she swore, pushing right back, trying to shove him off her. She thought she'd succeeded, but he managed to grab hold of her, and they both flipped over the edge of the pond.

She'd expected it to slope slowly downward, but instead it abruptly dropped off, and it was much deeper than she'd thought. Together, they sank down, and kept going, toward the muddy bottom.

Maggie twisted, trying to pull out of his grasp, but his other hand closed desperately around her arm, dragging her down with him. Her lungs screamed for air, and her eyes opened, filling instantly with water and grit.

She could make out Hoffmeier, not fighting to get back to the surface at all, just letting himself sink, trying to hold on to her.

Wrenching her legs in front of her body, she kicked hard, her feet connecting with his stomach. Air bubbles flooded all around her as his grip slipped, and she got free.

Knowing he wouldn't want to go down without her, Maggie swam hard for the surface, her muscles shaking now since she'd gone into the water without getting a breath. Finally, finally, she broke the surface.

She sucked in air over and over, coughing as she swam for the edge of the pond, not sure how they'd drifted so far so quickly. In the distance, she saw Clive running toward her.

She was close to the edge when he surfaced, gasping for air and grasping for her. His flailing arms gripped her hair, then slid down to the back of her neck as he pulled her under.

Maggie twisted frantically, turning to face him, and jammed her fist as hard as she could into his throat.

His eyes bulged, and his limbs thrashed as she watched him breathe in a mouthful of water.

She pushed for the surface, looking back in time to see his limbs slow then stop, and then he sank toward the bottom of the pond, his eyes and mouth wide and unmoving.

It was over. Maggie burst to the surface and gratefully drew in more air. She swam hard for the shore, until finally, her fingers dug into the dirt at the edge of the pond, and Clive was hauling her out of the water.

"Where's Hoffmeier?" he asked.

She blinked grit from her eyes and peered over the huge pond, toward the spot where he'd sunk. "He's gone."

"Good," Clive said. "Then we need to get back to the house. The medical helicopter is coming. Grant's in trouble."

"What?" She whipped her attention back to Clive.

"He lost a lot of blood. He needed a surgeon—and maybe a transfusion—ten minutes ago."

Maggie ran as fast as she could toward the house, still gasping for breath. Clive ran alongside her, and she could tell by his strides that she wasn't at her usual speed. She pushed harder, frantic to get back to Grant. She heard the roar of blades as the helicopter landed on the Hoffmeier estate's lawn.

Maggie watched two of her teammates race toward it, carrying an unconscious Grant between them. Nikki ran out after them, looking around until she spotted Maggie, then gestured for her sister to hurry.

Maggie ran faster, and Nikki gripped her arm, pushing her into the helicopter with Grant before it lifted off. The huge house faded below her, the forty-foot-wide pond soon becoming nothing more than a speck.

But Maggie barely noticed as she took Grant's limp hand in hers and sobbed, "You need to fight. I have something important to tell you, and you promised I'd get the chance as soon as this was all over."

Grant didn't move, his face and lips abnormally ashy, and Maggie held on tighter. "I love you," she said just as the monitor beside him let out a long, flat, final-sounding beep.

Epilogue

Maggie paced back and forth in the hospital waiting room until Nikki pushed her into a plastic chair.

"I should have stayed," Maggie said for what felt like the millionth time since they'd been in the Hoffmeier house two days ago. She'd gone over and over it in her mind, that moment she'd chosen to chase after Hoffmeier instead of staying beside Grant.

"He told you to go," Nikki reminded her. "So stop beating yourself up."

"She's right," Scott said, and Maggie glanced over at him, his hand clutching Chelsie's.

"You need to stop beating yourself up about all of it," Chelsie ordered. "And don't look at me like that. I'm fine."

Chelsie had been discharged a few hours earlier. She was moving more slowly, and she'd be off work for two weeks, but doctors didn't expect any lasting problems from her injury.

"Logan's fine, too," Ella put in, probably seeing guilt still on her face.

Maggie glanced from Ella to Logan, sitting close together on the uncomfortable hospital couch.

Logan nodded his agreement. "My injury just looked bad. But head wounds always bleed like crazy. And hey, we caught the three guys Hoffmeier paid off for those hits."

Maggie couldn't help smiling a little. Only someone in law enforcement could make light of having a bullet graze his head. But he was right—the injury itself had been minor, and he'd actually been released within a few hours.

"And it really worked out for me," Chelsie joked, wiggling her left hand, where a brand-new diamond sparkled.

Next to her, Scott rolled his eyes. "I already had the ring. But seeing you in the hospital, I just couldn't wait."

"See?" Nikki said. "Everyone is fine. And it's finally over."

"It will be," Maggie agreed.

Local police had dragged the Hoffmeier lake and found Jeff's body. And his family had been forcibly returned to DC to answer questions.

Apparently, Lorraine had been completely ignorant of her son's criminal activities. She'd simply thought he was spoiled and difficult. She'd had no idea he'd left DC ten years ago at her husband's insistence. She was back home in DC, cloistered alone in her house and avoiding the press camped out in her yard.

Frederik and Claudia were in custody, awaiting a hearing on bail. Clive predicted it would be denied, because of their resources and the amount of money they'd thrown at Jeff ten years ago, to make him go away. They were being charged as accessories in nine sexual assaults, and four assaults on law-enforcement officials, along with obstruction of justice, and a slew of other charges. Even if only some of them stuck, they'd pay.

Both had initially insisted they really thought Jeff had been in Europe the past ten years. But the Hoffmeiers were well-known in DC, and the story had broken quickly in the press. A witness had come forward, a friend of Claudia's from college, who'd said Claudia had tearfully confessed that she suspected her brother had raped Maggie. She'd confessed to telling her father, who'd changed the family logo and paid Jeff to stay away from them. Apparently, Claudia had gone back to that friend a few days later and said she was wrong, and that police had caught the real offender.

Back then, since Maggie was the first to be branded, and there were no other known victims, the friend had believed the story. Since Maggie's full name had always been kept out of the press accounts, she claimed she'd forgotten all about it until she saw the recent news.

Whether it was true or not, her going to police had broken Claudia's silence. There was some question to how much the Hoffmeier family actually knew, and how much they'd only suspected, but they'd known enough. They should have turned Jeff in a decade ago, and they could have prevented eight other women from going through what Maggie had. Instead, they'd changed the Hoffmeier Financial logo to get rid of the hook images that matched the brand on her neck. Instead, they had tried to protect the family business, and the family name.

Nikki squeezed her hand. "I talked to Mom and Dad this morning at the hotel. Apologized for telling them I was spending the week with friends, instead of letting them know I was coming here. I know they told you when they got here, but they are really proud of you, you know? For getting through this. For finding the guy and stopping him for good."

Maggie smiled back at her, but her feet tapped nervously on the floor of the surgical area waiting room. What was taking so long?

"He'll be here," Scott said.

Then the door to the waiting room opened, and he was. Maggie sensed everyone getting to their feet, but she couldn't be certain, because she was already running across the room. She stopped just in front of Grant, resisting the urge to throw her arms around his neck and just hang on and never let go.

He looked awful. His skin was still a little ashy, and pain was etched on his face, his right shoulder looking lumpy under his hospital gown from the bandages. The nurse pushed his wheelchair into the room and as soon as she left, he scolded, "Don't look at me like that. If all goes well, they'll release me tomorrow. I'll be kicking down doors with SWAT again in no time."

He winked at her, and Maggie felt a grin break free, then she did lean down and throw her arms around his neck, only lightly, barely touching him.

He squeezed back, with more strength than she'd expected after having his heart shocked back into rhythm on the helicopter, then being rushed here for a blood transfusion and surgery to repair his shoulder.

"How long?" she asked him, leaning back to look at his face.

"Probably six months," he replied. "The shoulder is going to need some rehabilitation."

Most SWAT agents would be furious at that much time away from the team, at the prospect of that much work to get back into fighting shape. But this was Grant, and he said it not only like a guarantee he'd do it, but with his typical good-natured attitude.

Nothing ever kept him down. It was one of the things she loved best about him.

At that moment, she realized he'd never even heard her say it. He'd almost died for her and Nikki, and he didn't really know how she felt about him.

She must have gone pale, because he said, "It's okay. I have a plan."

"What's your plan?" Scott asked him. "You taking some time off to heal, and having Clive hold the spot for you on the team?"

"Not exactly," Grant said, looking up at her.

He patted the chair next to where the nurse had left his wheelchair, and Maggie sat, as he folded her hand in his. It was funny how natural that already felt.

"You're not leaving SWAT?" she asked. "Because I—"

"No." He twisted a little in his chair so he was facing her. "But I talked to Martin two weeks ago." He was the leader of the second SWAT team at WFO. "One of his guys is transferring to the LA field office in April, and I asked about taking that spot."

"No," Maggie said. "You waited so long to get on a team. It's not fair that you be the one to—"

"I talked to Clive last week, too," he said. "I told him I wasn't going to be able to stay with the team. I didn't say why—I figured I'd wait until you and I talked about it first—but he knew."

Maggie blushed at the idea that the team already knew what was happening between her and Grant before she'd had the chance to tell them, but they were practically family. It shouldn't have surprised her. "Did Martin guarantee you a spot on his team?" She held her breath.

"No."

"Then I should be the one—"

"But he'll give it to me," Grant insisted. "As soon as I get through rehab and can prove to him my shoulder's back to one hundred percent." He brought her hand up to his lips and pressed a kiss to it. "It's perfect timing, Maggie. I should be through the rehab right when a spot opens up. I'll get it."

She grinned at him, not believing they might actually be able to date and still both have a place in SWAT. Although she'd miss running into missions with him by her side. "Are you sure?"

"I'm determined," he said. "I don't give up on something I want." He smiled back at her and asked, "It worked on you, didn't it?"

"Oh, yeah." She leaned in to kiss him, and just before her lips met his, she corrected, "But I think it was me who went after you until you couldn't resist any longer."

His mouth covered hers, showing her that determination. When he kissed her like that, she could almost forget he'd been shot. She could almost forget all of it. When he kissed her, there was a lightness in her soul that she'd never had before.

"Mmm," she mumbled against his mouth a few minutes later. "Don't ever stop that."

He smiled back at her, a glint in his eyes that promised he'd do more than that as soon as he healed up.

Suddenly remembering where they were, Maggie glanced over her shoulder and saw that everyone had cleared out to give them a little privacy.

But she didn't need it. She was ready to tell everyone, including the Bureau, that she and Grant were forming their own team now.

Before she could say it to him, he stroked his hand down her cheek and asked, "How are you doing?"

She knew exactly what he was asking. Four hours had passed while she'd waited frantically to hear about Grant's condition. Another two days had gone by while she sat in this waiting room with Scott, Nikki, Ella, Chelsie and Logan for Grant to be well enough to leave ICU.

Now it was September 1. A day she'd never thought

would be anything but painful, even after they'd finally caught Hoffmeier for good.

She squeezed his hand and told him honestly, "It's a good day today. A really good day."

He leaned down to kiss her again, and she pressed a finger to his lips. "You haven't let me finish what I was trying to tell you before," she told him softly.

Realization washed over his features, then a slow smile spread across his face, even before she said, "I love you, Grant."

Then he did kiss her again, and his lips were full of promise.

Today was the first day of a new start for her. A fresh new life with Grant, and she was going to grab hold with both hands and never let go.

* * * * *

COMING NEXT MONTH FROM

HARLEQUIN®

INTRIGUE

Available April 21, 2015

#1563 SHOWDOWN AT SHADOW JUNCTION
Big "D" Dads: The Daltons • by Joanna Wayne
When Jade Dalton escapes a ruthless kidnapper on the trail of a
multimillion-dollar necklace, Navy SEAL Booker Knox will do whatever
it takes to protect the beautiful event planner. Failure isn't an option.

#1564 TWO SOULS HOLLOW
The Gates • by Paula Graves
Ginny Coltrane might hold the key to proving Anson Daughtry's
innocence. But when Ginny is dragged into a drug war, Anson may be
her only hope of escaping with her life.

#1565 SCENE OF THE CRIME: KILLER COVE
by Carla Cassidy
Accused of murder, Bo McBride has finally returned to Lost Lagoon to
clear his name—with the help of sexy Claire Silver. But as they investigate,
it doesn't take long to realize that danger stalks Claire...

#1566 NAVY SEAL JUSTICE
Covert Cowboys, Inc. • by Elle James
After former Navy SEAL James Monahan and FBI agent Melissa Bradley's
mutual friend goes missing, they join forces to find him. But as a band of
dangerous criminals closes in, survival means trusting each other—their
toughest mission yet.

#1567 COWBOY INCOGNITO
The Brothers of Hastings Ridge Ranch • by Alice Sharpe
A roadtrip to uncover Zane Doe's identity exposes his *real* connection to
Kinsey Frost—and the murderous intentions of those once close to her. Now
Zane must protect her from someone who wants to silence her for good.

#1568 UNDER SUSPICION
Bayou Bonne Chance • by Mallory Kane
Undercover NSA agent Zach Winters vows to solve his best friend's
murder. With the criminals closing in, Zach will risk his own life to protect
a vulnerable widow and her beautiful bodyguard, Madeleine Tierney—the
woman he can't imagine saying goodbye to.

**YOU CAN FIND MORE INFORMATION ON UPCOMING HARLEQUIN® TITLES,
FREE EXCERPTS AND MORE AT WWW.HARLEQUIN.COM.**

HICNM0415

REQUEST YOUR FREE BOOKS!
2 FREE NOVELS PLUS 2 FREE GIFTS!

⟨H⟩ HARLEQUIN®

INTRIGUE®

BREATHTAKING ROMANTIC SUSPENSE

YES! Please send me 2 FREE Harlequin Intrigue® novels and my 2 FREE gifts (gifts are worth about $10). After receiving them, if I don't wish to receive any more books, I can return the shipping statement marked "cancel." If I don't cancel, I will receive 6 brand-new novels every month and be billed just $4.74 per book in the U.S. or $5.24 per book in Canada. That's a savings of at least 14% off the cover price! It's quite a bargain! Shipping and handling is just 50¢ per book in the U.S. and 75¢ per book in Canada.* I understand that accepting the 2 free books and gifts places me under no obligation to buy anything. I can always return a shipment and cancel at any time. Even if I never buy another book, the two free books and gifts are mine to keep forever.

182/382 HDN F42N

Name _____ (PLEASE PRINT)

Address _____ Apt. #

City _____ State/Prov. _____ Zip/Postal Code

Signature (if under 18, a parent or guardian must sign)

Mail to the Harlequin® Reader Service:
IN U.S.A.: P.O. Box 1867, Buffalo, NY 14240-1867
IN CANADA: P.O. Box 609, Fort Erie, Ontario L2A 5X3
Are you a subscriber to Harlequin Intrigue books
and want to receive the larger-print edition?
Call 1-800-873-8635 or visit www.ReaderService.com.

* Terms and prices subject to change without notice. Prices do not include applicable taxes. Sales tax applicable in N.Y. Canadian residents will be charged applicable taxes. Offer not valid in Quebec. This offer is limited to one order per household. Not valid for current subscribers to Harlequin Intrigue books. All orders subject to credit approval. Credit or debit balances in a customer's account(s) may be offset by any other outstanding balance owed by or to the customer. Please allow 4 to 6 weeks for delivery. Offer available while quantities last.

Your Privacy—The Harlequin® Reader Service is committed to protecting your privacy. Our Privacy Policy is available online at www.ReaderService.com or upon request from the Harlequin Reader Service.

We make a portion of our mailing list available to reputable third parties that offer products we believe may interest you. If you prefer that we not exchange your name with third parties, or if you wish to clarify or modify your communication preferences, please visit us at www.ReaderService.com/consumerschoice or write to us at Harlequin Reader Service Preference Service, P.O. Box 9062, Buffalo, NY 14269. Include your complete name and address.

HI13R

SPECIAL EXCERPT FROM

H HARLEQUIN

I N T R I G U E

*Bo McBride, accused but never arrested for the murder
of his girlfriend two years ago, has finally returned to
Lost Lagoon, Mississippi, to clear his name with
Claire Silber's help. But it doesn't take long for them
to realize that real danger stalks Claire.*

Read on for a sneak preview of
SCENE OF THE CRIME: KILLER COVE,
the latest crime scene book from
New York Times *bestselling author*
Carla Cassidy.

"So, your turn. Tell me what you've been doing for the last
two years," Claire asked. "Have you made yourself a new,
happy life? Found a new love? I heard through the grapevine
that you're living in Jackson now."

Bo nodded at the same time the sound of rain splattered
against the window. "I opened a little bar and grill, Bo's
Place, although it's nothing like the original." His dark
brows tugged together in a frown, as if remembering the
highly successful business he'd had here in town before he
was ostracized.

He took another big drink and then continued, "There's
no new woman in my life. I don't even have friends. Hell,
I'm not even sure what I'm doing here with you."

"You're here because I'm a bossy woman," she replied.
She got up to refill his glass. "And I thought you could use
an extra friend while you're here."

She handed him the fresh drink and then curled back up

in the corner of the sofa. The rain fell steadily now. She turned on the end table lamp as the room darkened with the storm.

For a few minutes they remained silent. She could tell by his distant stare toward the opposite wall that he was lost inside his head.

Despite his somber expression, she couldn't help but feel a physical attraction to him that she'd never felt before. Still, that wasn't what had driven her to seek contact with him, to invite him into her home. She had an ulterior motive.

A low rumble of thunder seemed to pull him out of his head. He focused on her and offered a small smile of apology. "Sorry about that. I got lost in thoughts of everything I need to get done before I leave town."

"I wanted to talk to you about that," she said.

He raised a dark brow. "About all the things I need to take care of?"

"No, about you leaving town."

"What about it?"

She drew a deep breath, knowing she was putting her nose in business that wasn't her own, and yet unable to stop herself. "Doesn't it bother you knowing that Shelly's murderer is still walking these streets, free as a bird?"

His eyes narrowed slightly. "Why are you so sure I'm innocent?" he asked.

Don't miss
SCENE OF THE CRIME: KILLER COVE
by New York Times *bestselling author Carla Cassidy,*
available May 2015 wherever
Harlequin® Intrigue books and ebooks are sold.

www.Harlequin.com

Copyright © 2015 by Carla Bracale

HIEXP0415

Love the Harlequin book you just read?

Your opinion matters.

Review this book on your favorite book site, review site, blog or your own social media properties and share your opinion with other readers!

Be sure to connect with us at:
Harlequin.com/Newsletters
Facebook.com/HarlequinBooks
Twitter.com/HarlequinBooks

JUST CAN'T GET ENOUGH?

Join our social communities
and talk to us online.

You will have access to the latest
news on upcoming titles and special
promotions, but most importantly,
you can talk to other fans about your
favorite Harlequin reads.

Harlequin.com/Community

Facebook.com/HarlequinBooks

Twitter.com/HarlequinBooks

Pinterest.com/HarlequinBooks

HSOCIAL

HARLEQUIN®

A Romance FOR EVERY MOOD™

**Stay up-to-date on all your
romance-reading news with the
Harlequin Shopping Guide,
featuring bestselling authors, exciting new
miniseries, books to watch and more!**

The newest issue will be delivered right to you
with our compliments! There are 4 each year.

Signing up is easy.

EMAIL

ShoppingGuide@Harlequin.ca

WRITE TO US

HARLEQUIN BOOKS
Attention: Customer Service Department
P.O. Box 9057, Buffalo, NY 14269-9057

OR PHONE

1-800-873-8635 in the United States
1-888-343-9777 in Canada

Please allow 4-6 weeks for delivery of the first issue by mail.

THE WORLD IS BETTER WITH

Romance

Harlequin has everything from contemporary, passionate and heartwarming to suspenseful and inspirational stories.

Whatever your mood, we have a romance just for you!

Connect with us to find your next great read, special offers and more.

f /HarlequinBooks

🐦 @HarlequinBooks

www.HarlequinBlog.com

www.Harlequin.com/Newsletters

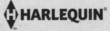

◆ HARLEQUIN®

A *Romance* FOR EVERY MOOD™

www.Harlequin.com

SERIESHALOAD2015